HORROR

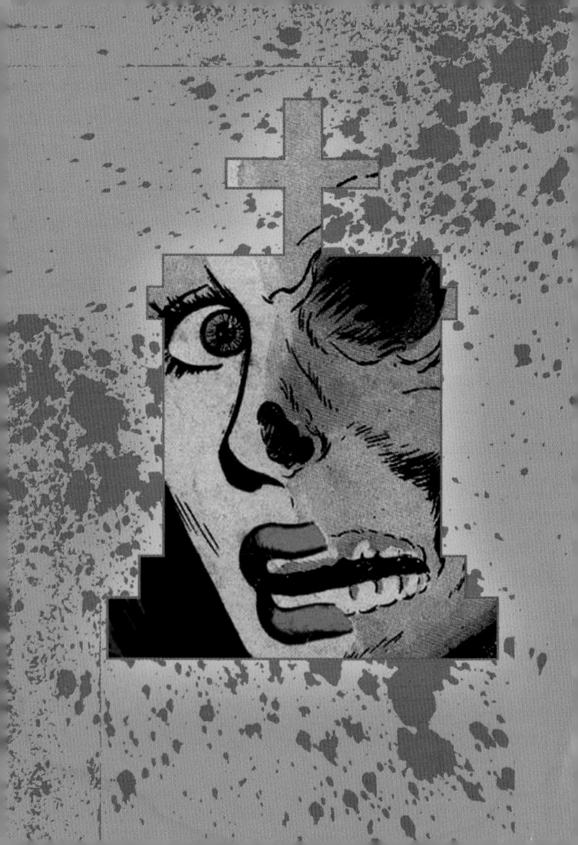

LITTLE BOOK OF VINTAGE

HORROR

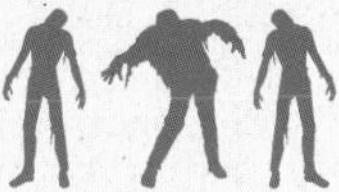

TIM PILCHER

ILEX

LITTLE BOOK OF VINTAGE: HORROR

First published in the UK, US, and Canada
in 2012 by
I L E X
210 High Street
Lewes
East Sussex BN7 2NS, UK
www.ilex-press.com

Publisher: Alastair Campbell
Creative Director: James Hollywell
Managing Editor: Nick Jones
Senior Editor: Ellie Wilson
Commissioning Editor: Tim Pilcher
Art Director: Julie Weir
Designer: Simon Goggin

British Library Cataloguing-in-Publication Data
A catalogue record for this book is available from the British Library.

ISBN: 978-1-908150-36-3

Printed and bound in China

Colour Origination by Ivy Press Reprographics

10 9 8 7 6 5 4 3 2 1

Shlop font courtesy of Ray Larabie
www.larabiefonts.com
Zombie icons courtesy of Ben Johnson
http://benblogged.com/
and Jean-Benoist Prouveur
http://membres.multimania.fr/grositez/

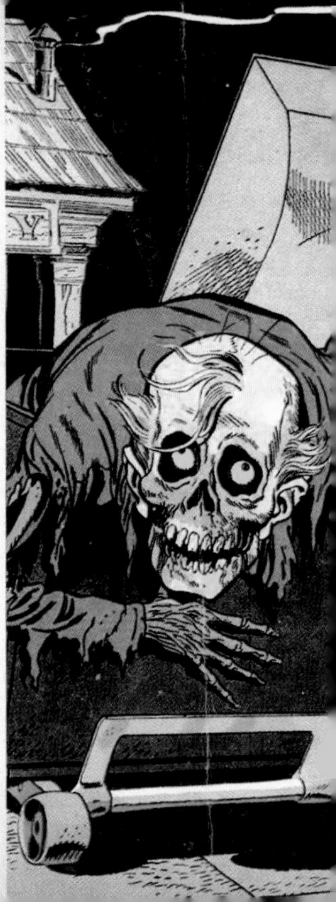

CONTENTS

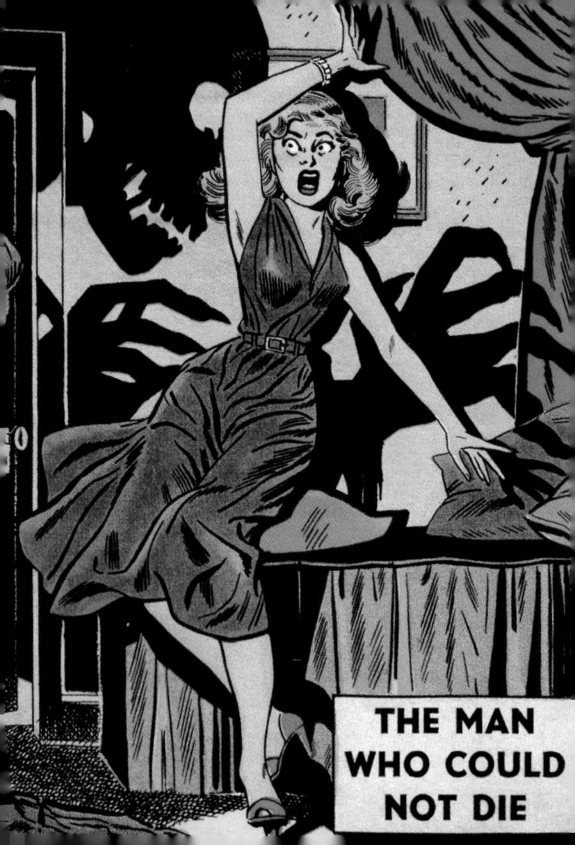
THE MAN WHO COULD NOT DIE

INTRODUCTION

"You have come from the outer world . . . you have crossed the scorching infernos . . . you have entered the realm of mystery . . ." Thus, typically, began an issue of *Chamber of Chills*, a classic horror comic published in 1952.

Like so many of the comic book genres, horror had its roots in the "spicy" pulp magazines like *Terror Tales* and *Horror Stories* of the 1920s and 1930s. These stories often had young women molested by "weird menaces" and mad scientists bent on world domination via their perverted creations.

While many early detective and superhero anthology comics of the Thirties and Forties featured the odd supernatural story, it wasn't until Avon Publications released *Eerie Comics* #1 (January 1947) that a complete horror comic—from front to back—first appeared. The cover featured a red-eyed, pointy-eared ghoul threatening a bound beauty in a scanty red evening gown. This anthology had six occult tales including *The Man-Eating Lizards* drawn by a young Joe Kubert. Strangely, after this first issue, the title went dormant for four years, reappearing in 1951 as *Eerie*, beginning with a new #1 and running for 17 issues.

It took another year before the first ongoing horror comic series, *Adventures into the Unknown*, would appear in Fall 1948. Simultaneously EC Comics—which would become the most prominent horror-comics publisher of the 1950s—published its first horror story, *Zombie Terror*, by a then-unknown writer and artist, Johnny Craig, in the superhero comic *Moon Girl* #5. Craig and EC would become synonymous with horror comics in the early Fifties.

But the floodgates really flew open the following year, with the first horror comics from Atlas Comics. Like many publishers, Atlas turned many of their superhero and crime comics into full blown horror titles, including *Marvel Mystery Comics*, which became *Marvel Tales* with #93 (August 1949). Harvey Comics quickly followed, changing its superhero title *Black Cat* into the horror comic *Black Cat Mystery* with issue #30 (August 1951).

But the undisputed publishing king of Fifties horror was EC Comics. Their grim 'n' grisly titles like *Vault of Horror*, *Tales from the Crypt*, and *Haunt of Fear* became instant classics with fantastic art by Jack Davis, Johnny Craig, Graham Ingels, and Jack Cole.

Many comics featured "horror hosts," such as the Crypt Keeper or Dr. Death, who would introduce the stories and often finish off the tale with a word of warning for the readers, lest they emulate the shocking acts inside. Grave robbers, murderers, and philanderers all got their comeuppances in ever inventive and increasingly grisly endings.

Tragically, this thriving genre collapsed in 1954 with the "great comic purge" led by child psychologist—and author of *Seduction of the Innocent*—Dr. Fredric Wertham and Senator Estes Kefauver. During one fateful Senate Subcommittee hearing into how horror comics allegedly encouraged juvenile delinquency, EC Comics' publisher William Gaines was publically humiliated, and the hearings—to all intents

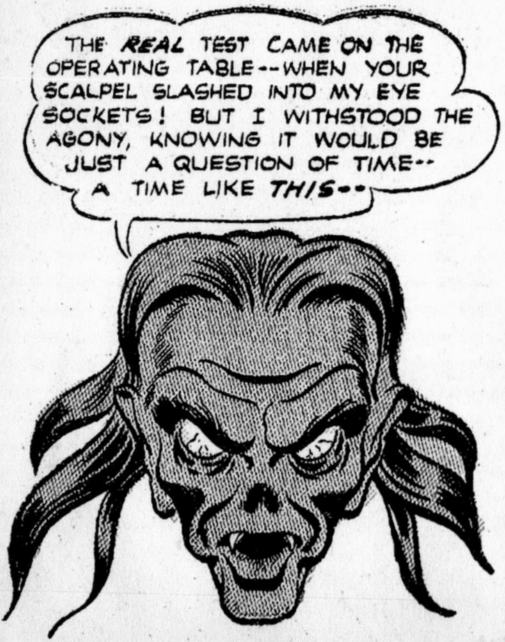
THE *REAL* TEST CAME ON THE OPERATING TABLE--WHEN YOUR SCALPEL SLASHED INTO MY EYE SOCKETS! BUT I WITHSTOOD THE AGONY, KNOWING IT WOULD BE JUST A QUESTION OF TIME-- A TIME LIKE *THIS*--

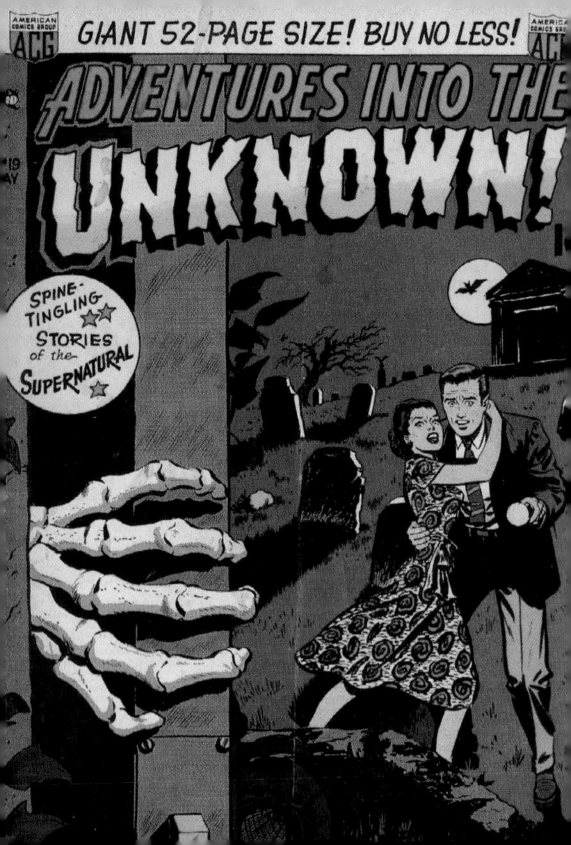
AMERICAN COMICS GROUP
ACG
GIANT 52-PAGE SIZE! BUY NO LESS!
ADVENTURES INTO THE
UNKNOWN!
SPINE-TINGLING STORIES of the SUPERNATURAL

and purposes—destroyed the company. Rather than face government intervention, the comics industry instigated a self-imposed strict regulatory body, the Comics Code Authority (CCA).

Once the Comics Code had been introduced, horror comics were effectively neutered. No longer could they feature the words "crime," "horror," or "terror" in their titles. Not only were "all scenes of horror, excessive bloodshed, gory or gruesome crimes, depravity, lust, sadism, masochism" not permitted, but neither were "scenes dealing with, or instruments associated with walking dead, torture, vampires and vampirism, ghouls, cannibalism, and werewolfism . . ." making horror comics impossible to publish. The Golden Age of horror comics was over.

Within these pages you'll find classic strips and art from a bygone era. Artists attacked by their paintings and sculptures; musicians making deals with the devil; and beautiful vamps leading unwitting fools to their doom!

And for those who are more exotically inclined, there are seductive snake-god priestesses, strange animal cults, voodoo witch doctors, cannibals, and tribes looking for their next shrunken-head trophy. So beware! The evil that men do lives on these pages. Turn them at your peril.

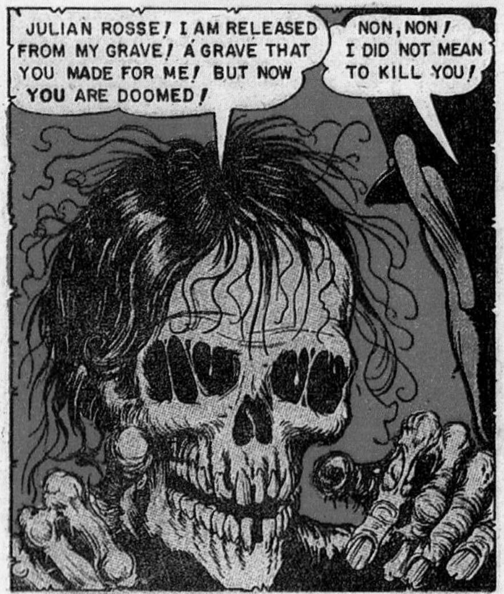
JULIAN ROSSE! I AM RELEASED FROM MY GRAVE! A GRAVE THAT YOU MADE FOR ME! BUT NOW YOU ARE DOOMED!
NON, NON! I DID NOT MEAN TO KILL YOU!

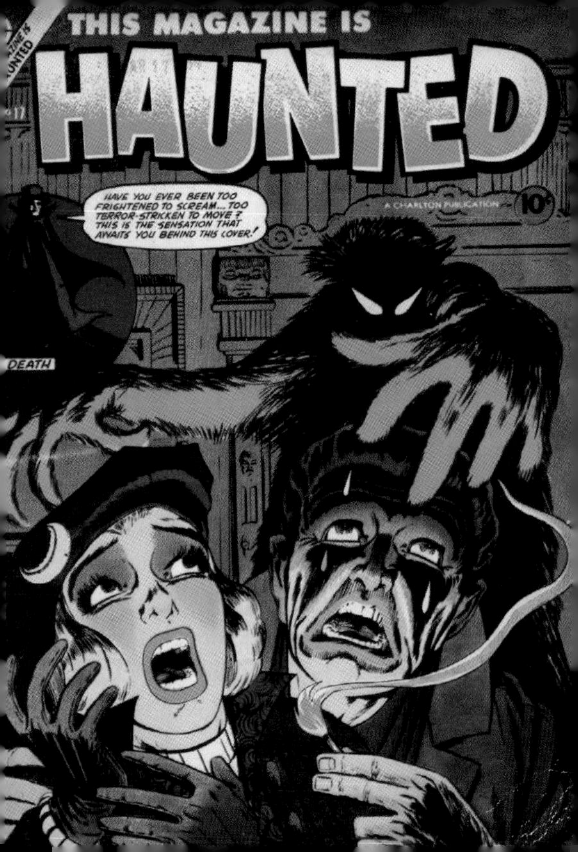
THIS MAGAZINE IS
HAUNTED
HAVE YOU EVER BEEN TOO FRIGHTENED TO SCREAM... TOO TERROR-STRICKEN TO MOVE? THIS IS THE SENSATION THAT AWAITS YOU BEHIND THIS COVER!
A CHARLTON PUBLICATION
10¢
DEATH

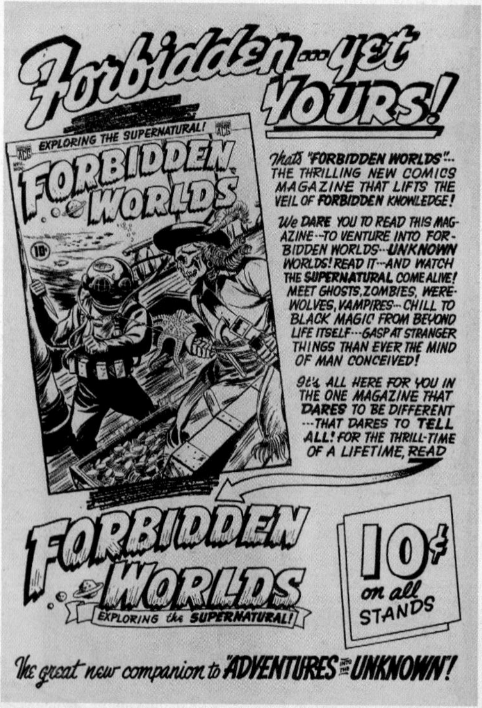
Forbidden...yet YOURS!
EXPLORING THE SUPERNATURAL!
FORBIDDEN WORLDS
10¢
That's "FORBIDDEN WORLDS"... THE THRILLING NEW COMICS MAGAZINE THAT LIFTS THE VEIL OF FORBIDDEN KNOWLEDGE!
We DARE YOU TO READ THIS MAGAZINE--TO VENTURE INTO FORBIDDEN WORLDS---UNKNOWN WORLDS! READ IT---AND WATCH THE SUPERNATURAL COME ALIVE! MEET GHOSTS, ZOMBIES, WEREWOLVES, VAMPIRES---CHILL TO BLACK MAGIC FROM BEYOND LIFE ITSELF---GASP AT STRANGER THINGS THAN EVER THE MIND OF MAN CONCEIVED!
It's ALL HERE FOR YOU IN THE ONE MAGAZINE THAT DARES TO BE DIFFERENT ---THAT DARES TO TELL ALL! FOR THE THRILL-TIME OF A LIFETIME, READ
FORBIDDEN WORLDS
EXPLORING the SUPERNATURAL!
10¢ on all STANDS
The great new companion to "ADVENTURES INTO THE UNKNOWN"!

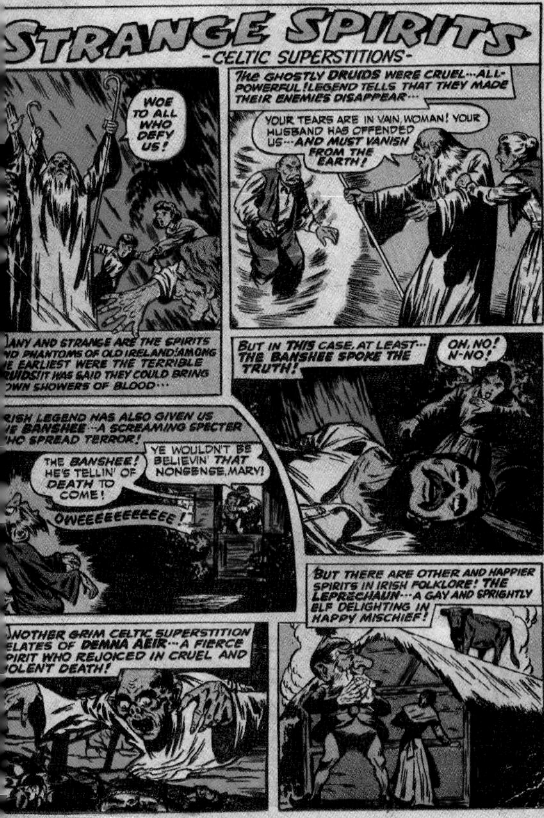
STRANGE SPIRITS
-CELTIC SUPERSTITIONS-
WOE TO ALL WHO DEFY US!
ANY AND STRANGE ARE THE SPIRITS ND PHANTOMS OF OLD IRELAND! AMONG E EARLIEST WERE THE TERRIBLE RUIDS! IT WAS SAID THEY COULD BRING OWN SHOWERS OF BLOOD...
THE GHOSTLY DRUIDS WERE CRUEL...ALL-POWERFUL! LEGEND TELLS THAT THEY MADE THEIR ENEMIES DISAPPEAR...
YOUR TEARS ARE IN VAIN, WOMAN! YOUR HUSBAND HAS OFFENDED US...AND MUST VANISH FROM THE EARTH!
RISH LEGEND HAS ALSO GIVEN US E BANSHEE...A SCREAMING SPECTER HO SPREAD TERROR!
THE BANSHEE! HE'S TELLIN' OF DEATH TO COME!
YE WOULDN'T BE BELIEVIN' THAT NONSENSE, MARY!
OWEEEEEEEEEEE!
BUT IN THIS CASE, AT LEAST... THE BANSHEE SPOKE THE TRUTH!
OH, NO! N-NO!
NOTHER GRIM CELTIC SUPERSTITION ELATES OF DEMNA AEIR...A FIERCE PIRIT WHO REJOICED IN CRUEL AND IOLENT DEATH!
BUT THERE ARE OTHER AND HAPPIER SPIRITS IN IRISH FOLKLORE! THE LEPRECHAUN...A GAY AND SPRIGHTLY ELF DELIGHTING IN HAPPY MISCHIEF!

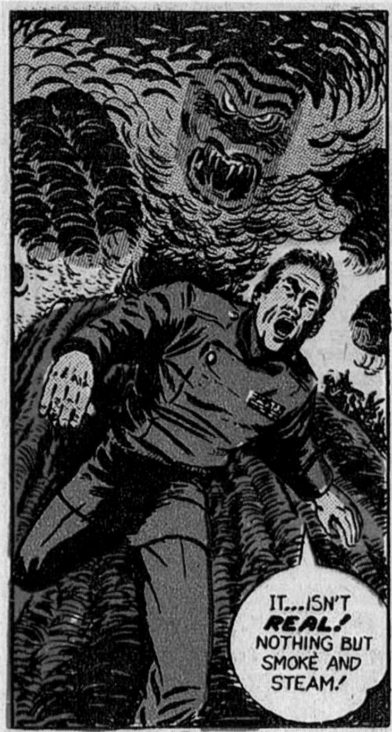
IT...ISN'T
REAL!
NOTHING BUT
SMOKE AND
STEAM!

King of the ZOMBIES

IN THE YEAR 1847, the mighty empire of Spain looked calculatingly towards its Caribbean principality of Costabara and decided that this great tropical island contributed too little towards the royal coffers. What was needed was a Spanish overlord who would organize the island into a producing kingdom by teaching the natives that they must work for the great nation across the seas. And so Juan Montevaldo was chosen as the first white king of Costabara.

The rulers of Spain knew what they were doing in their choice. Montevaldo was a harsh man . . . a stern taskmaster who knew no fear. He showed this from the first in pressing the natives into slave labor gangs that would work for Spain and Spain alone. What matter if whips were needed to keep up production . . . or if the workers died beneath the ordeal? Yet, despite its cruelty, it could not be said that Montevaldo was entirely successful. The work quotas he had set were not being met . . . why? Investigation soon produced the answer. The natives felt they owed their loyalty, not to Spain or to the white man who now ruled over them as king, but to their ancient tribal god, Obada . . . he who had the power to raise the dead and make them walk abroad. And so, by the thousands, they escaped from the work gangs and made their way deep into the jungle vastnesses, where they sought refuge with old Kalomna, the voodoo witch doctor who was Obada's mortal intermediary.

Montevaldo knew that if ever he was to break the voodoo grip over the natives, it must be through Kalomna. And so he sent a large detachment of Spanish troops into the jungle, and the surprise daring of this move paid off. Kalomna was captured and brought to civilization. There Montevaldo, the king, set to work. He began by offering princely rewards if the old man would order the natives to stop deserting and give their all in Spanish service. But Kalomna refused, and continued to refuse. Cruelly, Montevaldo ordered punishment . . . but neither flogging nor the most horrible tortures could make the aged witch doctor accede. And so, in the public square, with thousands of natives forced to look on, King Montevaldo ordered the old man to be burned at the stake.

It was over now . . . the awful deed was done! And now that Kalomna had been taught a lesson, it was time that the slaves assembled at this spot learn theirs, too. Turning to the captain of his guards, the king pointed imperiously to the assembled populace. "Fire!" he cried. But the order was never put into effect. Suddenly, a mighty cry went up from the onlookers. "Obada!" they shrieked. *"Obada!"*

Wheeling, Montevaldo recoiled in horror. For, over the blackened ashes of what once had been the old witch doctor, a terrible form was materializing . . . a giant and towering figure whose stern countenance bespoke the imminence of a mighty revenge. It couldn't be true . . . it was all part of this mumbo-jumbo and trickery! But even as he tried to convince himself of this, the white king saw something else. Brooding above the dead form of his former high priest, Obada stretched forth a hand. And the blackened ashes seemed to leap together and gain frightening life . . . in the image of old Kalomna! And Montevaldo's limbs were paralyzed with a strange fear as the charred hulk moved toward him . . . closer . . . *closer!* "Get back!" the white man cried. *"I'm king here . . . obey me!"*

The blackened lips moved. "You *were* king!" they intoned. "Now let your fate be that which your cruelty has ordained!" The thing which had once been a man raised its arms. What came then was some form of incantation, weird and inexpressibly old. Listening, King Montevaldo felt a strange stiffening invading his bones, his very joints. Something seemed to be glazing his eyes, closing off his power to think. All he knew was that the master called . . . and he must follow!

The figure of Obada, god of voodoo, was fading now, and old Kalomna had returned to the ashes from which he had arisen. And rigidly, Montevaldo stalked forward, his eyes blind and blank as he clumped toward the jungle with the mechanical tread of the undead. For he was king only of the zombies now!

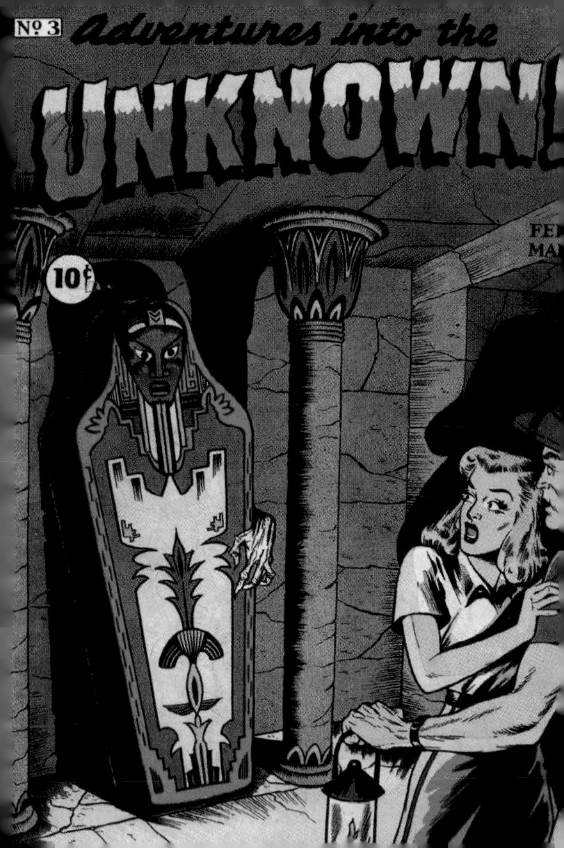

Nº 3
Adventures into the
UNKNOWN
10¢

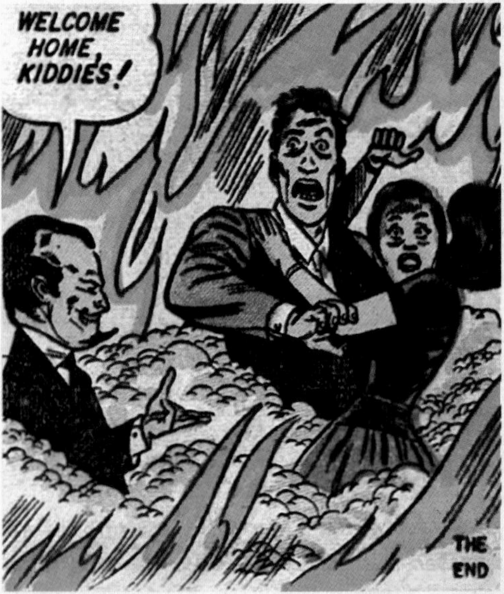
WELCOME HOME, KIDDIES!
THE END

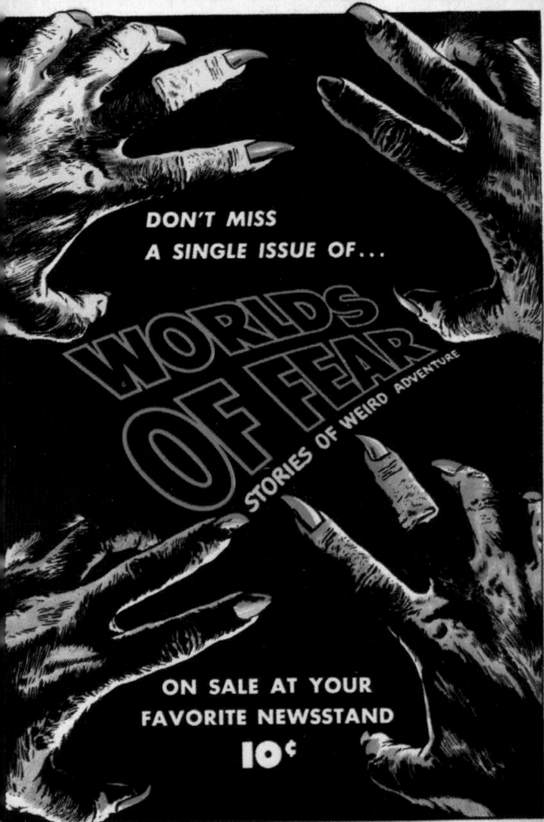
DON'T MISS
A SINGLE ISSUE OF...
WORLDS OF FEAR
STORIES OF WEIRD ADVENTURE
ON SALE AT YOUR
FAVORITE NEWSSTAND
10¢

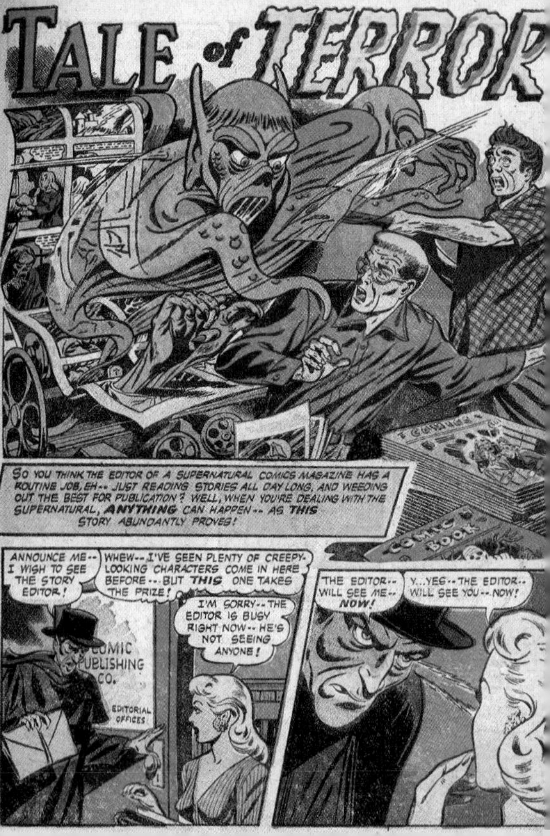
TALE of TERROR
SO YOU THINK THE EDITOR OF A SUPERNATURAL COMICS MAGAZINE HAS A ROUTINE JOB, EH-- JUST READING STORIES ALL DAY LONG, AND WEEDING OUT THE BEST FOR PUBLICATION? WELL, WHEN YOU'RE DEALING WITH THE SUPERNATURAL, ANYTHING CAN HAPPEN -- AS THIS STORY ABUNDANTLY PROVES!
COMIC BOOK
ANNOUNCE ME-- I WISH TO SEE THE STORY EDITOR!
WHEW-- I'VE SEEN PLENTY OF CREEPY-LOOKING CHARACTERS COME IN HERE BEFORE -- BUT THIS ONE TAKES THE PRIZE!
I'M SORRY-- THE EDITOR IS BUSY RIGHT NOW -- HE'S NOT SEEING ANYONE!
COMIC PUBLISHING CO.
EDITORIAL OFFICES
THE EDITOR-- WILL SEE ME-- NOW!
Y...YES-- THE EDITOR-- WILL SEE YOU -- NOW!

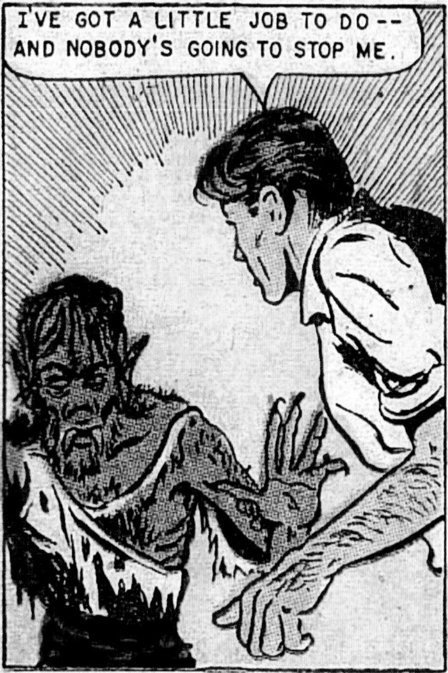
I'VE GOT A LITTLE JOB TO DO -- AND NOBODY'S GOING TO STOP ME.

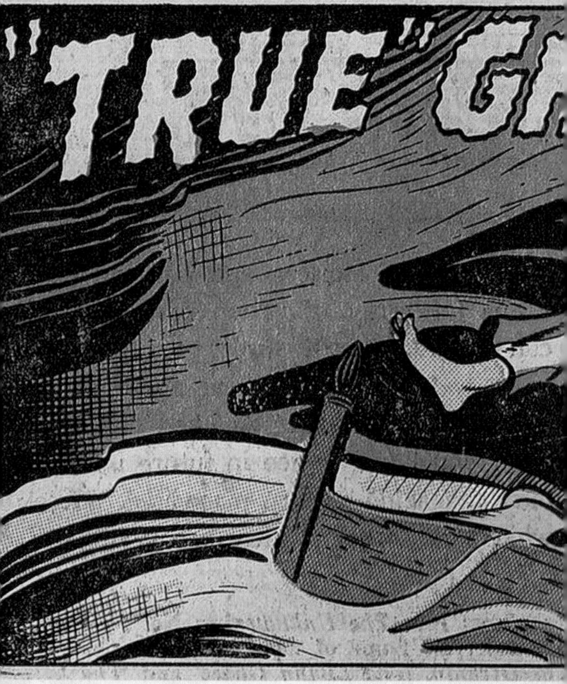
"TRUE"

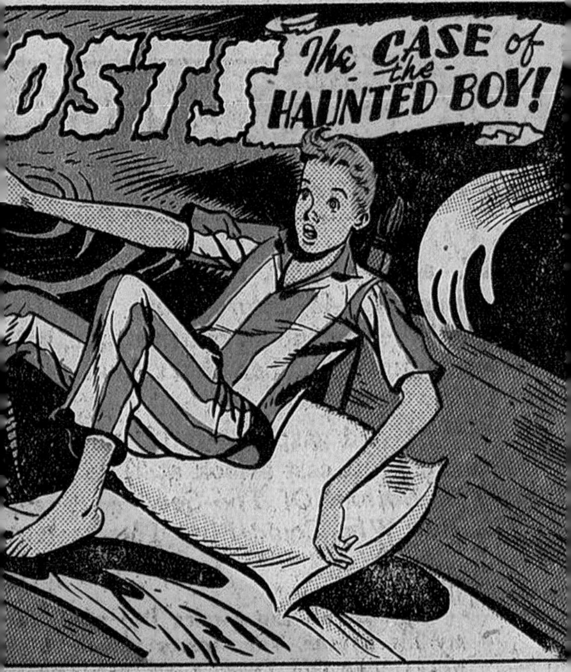
OSTS
The CASE of the HAUNTED BOY!

BY FAR THE STRANGEST STORY OF 1949 WAS THE **CASE OF THE HAUNTED BOY!** IN WASHINGTON, D.C., STRANGE "SPIRITS" BEGAN TO HARASS A 14-YEAR-OLD BOY, UNTIL THE CASE WAS FINALLY INVESTIGATED BY THE SOCIETY FOR PARAPSYCHOLOGY AND DUKE UNIVERSITY! THE CASE AMAZED AND PUZZLED EVERYONE EXCEPT THE HAUNTED BOY --- **WHO REMAINED HAUNTED!**

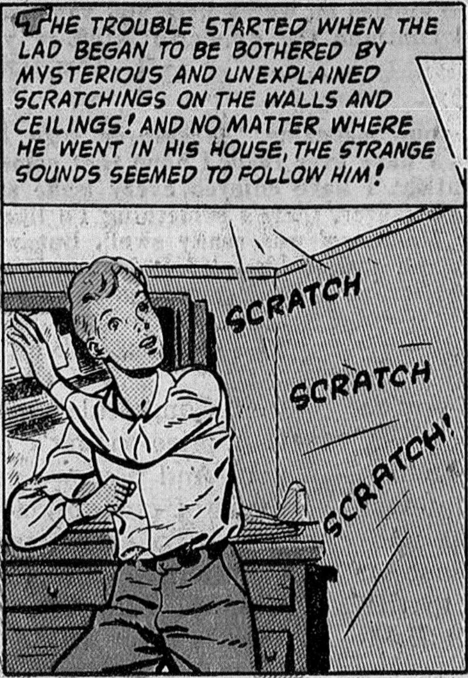
THE TROUBLE STARTED WHEN THE LAD BEGAN TO BE BOTHERED BY MYSTERIOUS AND UNEXPLAINED SCRATCHINGS ON THE WALLS AND CEILINGS! AND NO MATTER WHERE HE WENT IN HIS HOUSE, THE STRANGE SOUNDS SEEMED TO FOLLOW HIM!
SCRATCH
SCRATCH
SCRATCH!

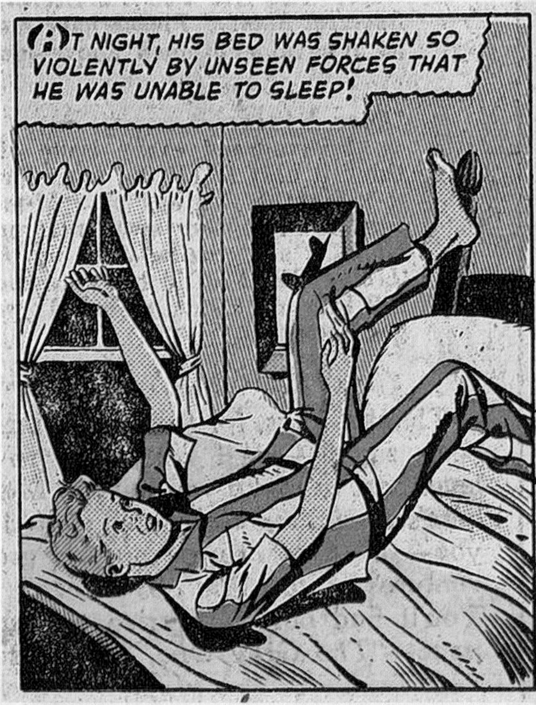
AT NIGHT, HIS BED WAS SHAKEN SO VIOLENTLY BY UNSEEN FORCES THAT HE WAS UNABLE TO SLEEP!

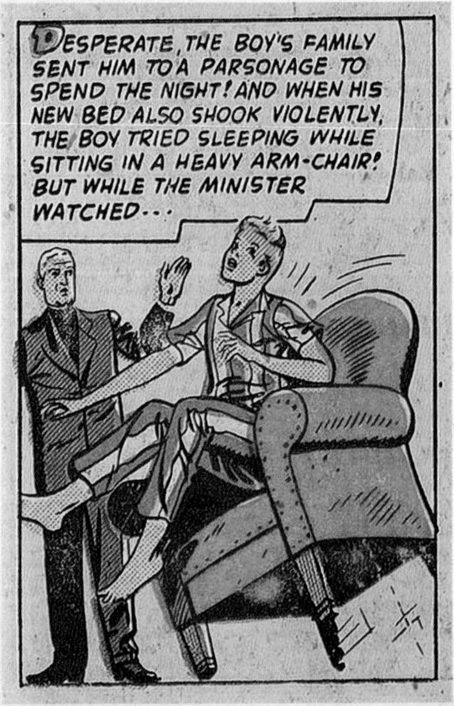
DESPERATE, THE BOY'S FAMILY SENT HIM TO A PARSONAGE TO SPEND THE NIGHT! AND WHEN HIS NEW BED ALSO SHOOK VIOLENTLY, THE BOY TRIED SLEEPING WHILE SITTING IN A HEAVY ARM-CHAIR! BUT WHILE THE MINISTER WATCHED...

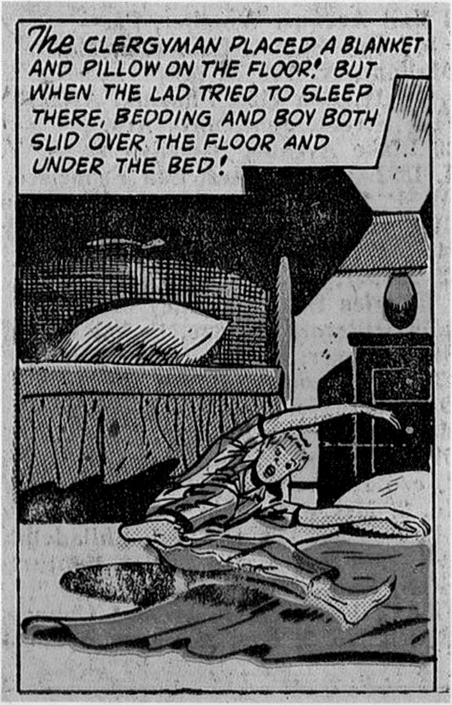
THE CLERGYMAN PLACED A BLANKET AND PILLOW ON THE FLOOR! BUT WHEN THE LAD TRIED TO SLEEP THERE, BEDDING AND BOY BOTH SLID OVER THE FLOOR AND UNDER THE BED!

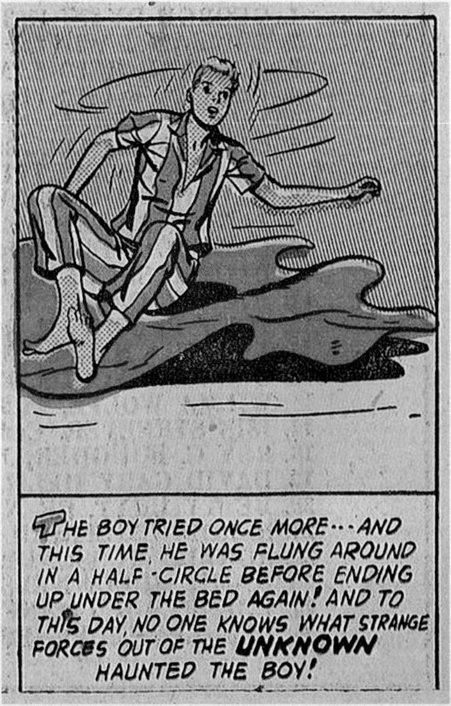
THE BOY TRIED ONCE MORE···AND THIS TIME, HE WAS FLUNG AROUND IN A HALF-CIRCLE BEFORE ENDING UP UNDER THE BED AGAIN! AND TO THIS DAY, NO ONE KNOWS WHAT STRANGE FORCES OUT OF THE UNKNOWN HAUNTED THE BOY!

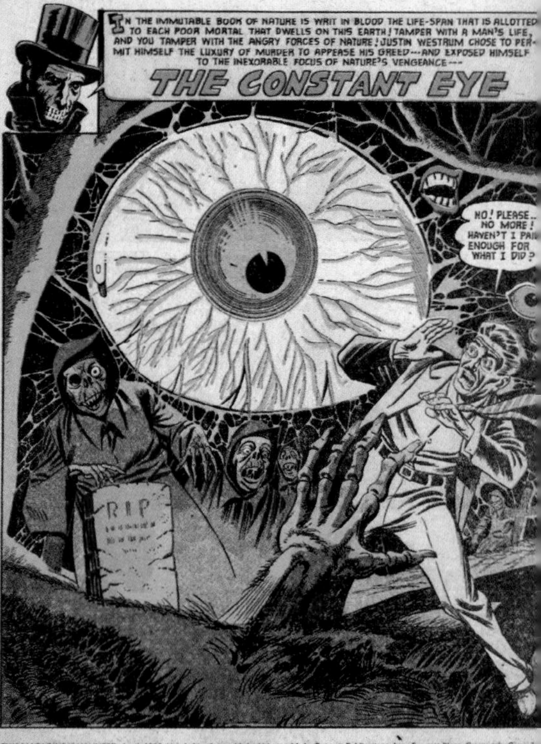
IN THE IMMUTABLE BOOK OF NATURE IS WRIT IN BLOOD THE LIFE-SPAN THAT IS ALLOTTED TO EACH POOR MORTAL THAT DWELLS ON THIS EARTH! TAMPER WITH A MAN'S LIFE, AND YOU TAMPER WITH THE ANGRY FORCES OF NATURE! JUSTIN WESTRUM CHOSE TO PERMIT HIMSELF THE LUXURY OF MURDER TO APPEASE HIS GREED---AND EXPOSED HIMSELF TO THE INEXORABLE FOCUS OF NATURE'S VENGEANCE---
THE CONSTANT EYE
NO! PLEASE... NO MORE! HAVEN'T I PAI ENOUGH FOR WHAT I DID?
R.I.P.

THIS MAGAZINE IS HAUNTED, April, 1952, Vol. 1, No. 4, is published bi-monthly by Fawcett Publications, Inc., Fawcett Place, Greenwich, Conn. S class entry applied for at the post office, Greenwich, Conn. Additional entry applied for at Louisville, Ky. Copyright 1951 by Fawcett Publications Editorial and advertising offices, 67 W. 44th St., N. Y. 18, N. Y. Send remittances and letters concerning subscriptions, change of address, etc., to C lation Dept., Fawcett Pl., Greenwich, Conn. Subscription rate 12 issues for $1.20 in U. S., possessions and Canada. Foreign, $1.70 in international r order, U. S. funds. Printed in U. S. A.

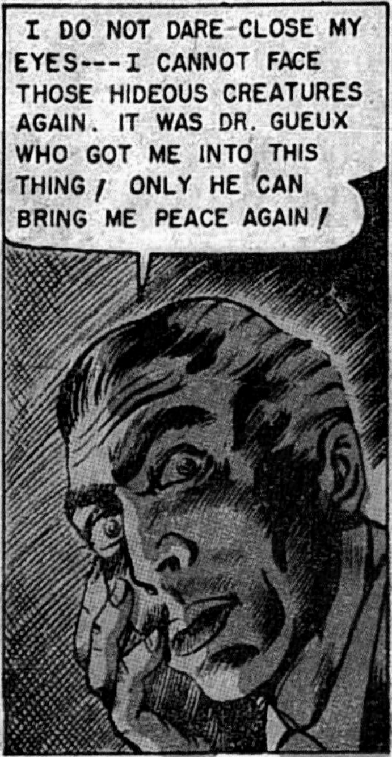
I DO NOT DARE CLOSE MY EYES---I CANNOT FACE THOSE HIDEOUS CREATURES AGAIN. IT WAS DR. GUEUX WHO GOT ME INTO THIS THING! ONLY HE CAN BRING ME PEACE AGAIN!

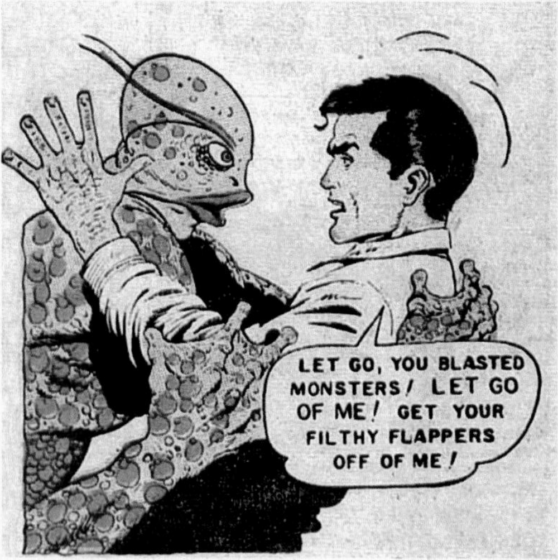
LET GO, YOU BLASTED MONSTERS! LET GO OF ME! GET YOUR FILTHY FLAPPERS OFF OF ME!

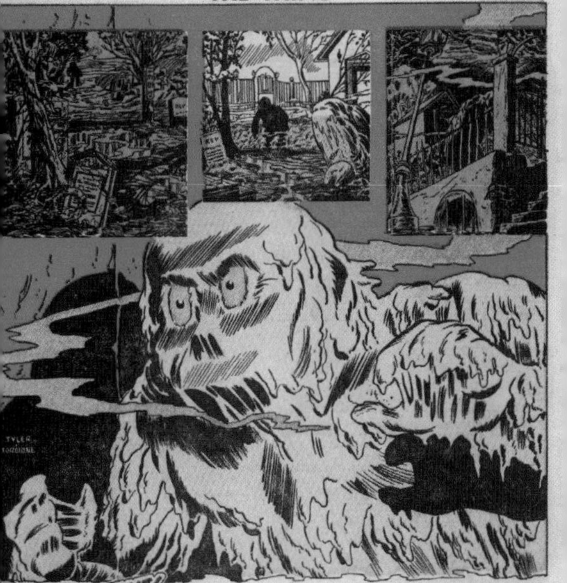

THE "THING" PRESENTS

THE CREATURE

FROM DIMENSION 2-K-31

AGGHH! HORRIBLE! A MONSTROSITY! GHASTLY... THESE WERE THE WORDS USED WHEN THEY REFERRED TO THIS *THING*... THE PHENOMENAL RESULT OF DR. EUSTUS RIKO'S EXPERIMENT TO PIERCE INTO A NEW EXISTENCE! YES, BEHOLD THE FORMLESS MASS AS IT APPROACHES... ***THIS IS THE CREATURE...*** AND THIS IS THE STORY OF THE ***CREATURE...***

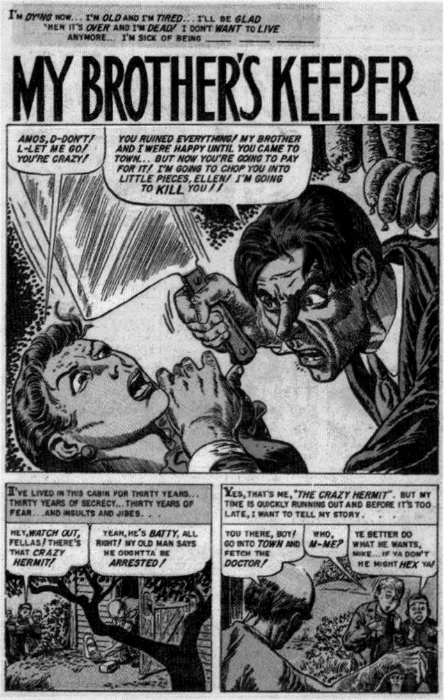
I'M DYING NOW... I'M OLD AND I'M TIRED... I'LL BE GLAD WHEN IT'S OVER AND I'M DEAD! I DON'T WANT TO LIVE ANYMORE... I'M SICK OF BEING ____ ____ ____
MY BROTHER'S KEEPER
AMOS, D-DON'T! L-LET ME GO! YOU'RE CRAZY!
YOU RUINED EVERYTHING! MY BROTHER AND I WERE HAPPY UNTIL YOU CAME TO TOWN... BUT NOW YOU'RE GOING TO PAY FOR IT! I'M GOING TO CHOP YOU INTO LITTLE PIECES, ELLEN! I'M GOING TO KILL YOU!!
I'VE LIVED IN THIS CABIN FOR THIRTY YEARS... THIRTY YEARS OF SECRECY... THIRTY YEARS OF FEAR... AND INSULTS AND JIBES. . .
HEY, WATCH OUT, FELLAS! THERE'S THAT CRAZY HERMIT!
YEAH, HE'S BATTY, ALL RIGHT! MY OLD MAN SAYS HE OUGHTTA BE ARRESTED!
YES, THAT'S ME, "THE CRAZY HERMIT". BUT MY TIME IS QUICKLY RUNNING OUT AND BEFORE IT'S TOO LATE, I WANT TO TELL MY STORY. . .
YOU THERE, BOY! GO INTO TOWN AND FETCH THE DOCTOR!
WHO, M-ME?
YE BETTER DO WHAT HE WANTS, MIKE... IF YA DON'T HE MIGHT HEX YA!

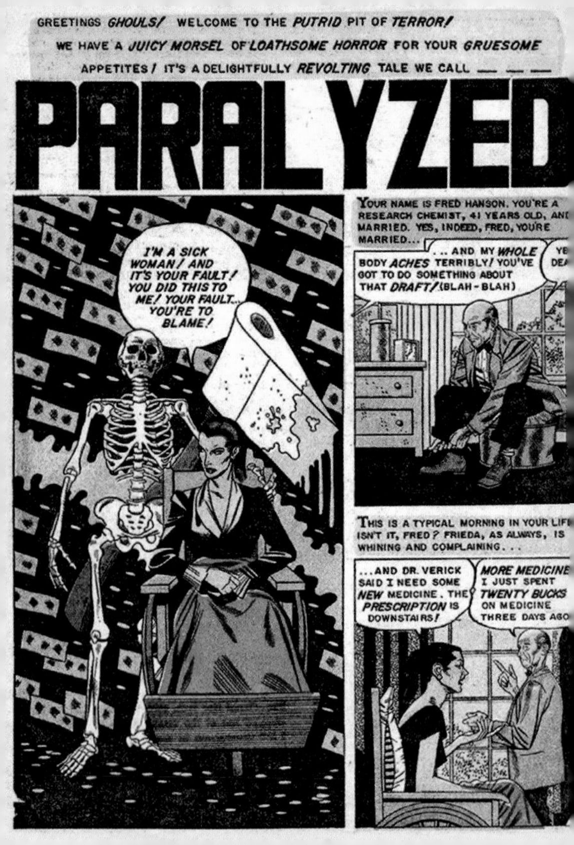
GREETINGS GHOULS! WELCOME TO THE PUTRID PIT OF TERROR!
WE HAVE A JUICY MORSEL OF LOATHSOME HORROR FOR YOUR GRUESOME APPETITES! IT'S A DELIGHTFULLY REVOLTING TALE WE CALL — — —
PARALYZED
I'M A SICK WOMAN! AND IT'S YOUR FAULT! YOU DID THIS TO ME! YOUR FAULT... YOU'RE TO BLAME!
YOUR NAME IS FRED HANSON. YOU'RE A RESEARCH CHEMIST, 41 YEARS OLD, AND MARRIED. YES, INDEED, FRED, YOU'RE MARRIED...
... AND MY WHOLE BODY ACHES TERRIBLY! YOU'VE GOT TO DO SOMETHING ABOUT THAT DRAFT! (BLAH - BLAH)
THIS IS A TYPICAL MORNING IN YOUR LIFE ISN'T IT, FRED? FRIEDA, AS ALWAYS, IS WHINING AND COMPLAINING...
...AND DR. VERICK SAID I NEED SOME NEW MEDICINE. THE PRESCRIPTION IS DOWNSTAIRS!
MORE MEDICINE! I JUST SPENT TWENTY BUCKS ON MEDICINE THREE DAYS AGO

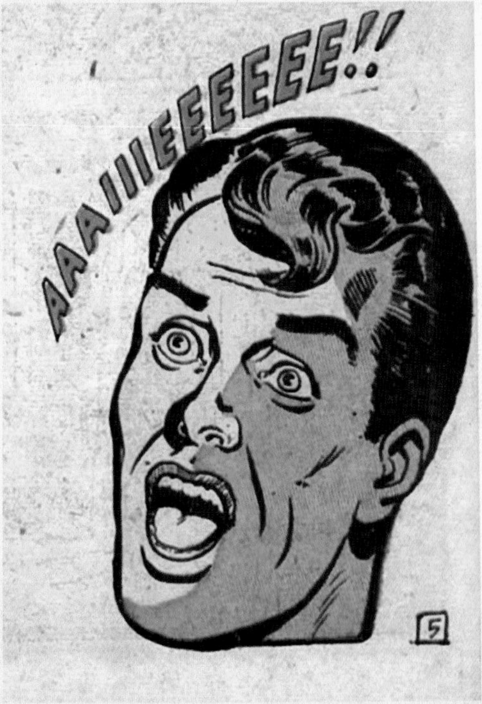
AAAIIIEEEEEE!!
S

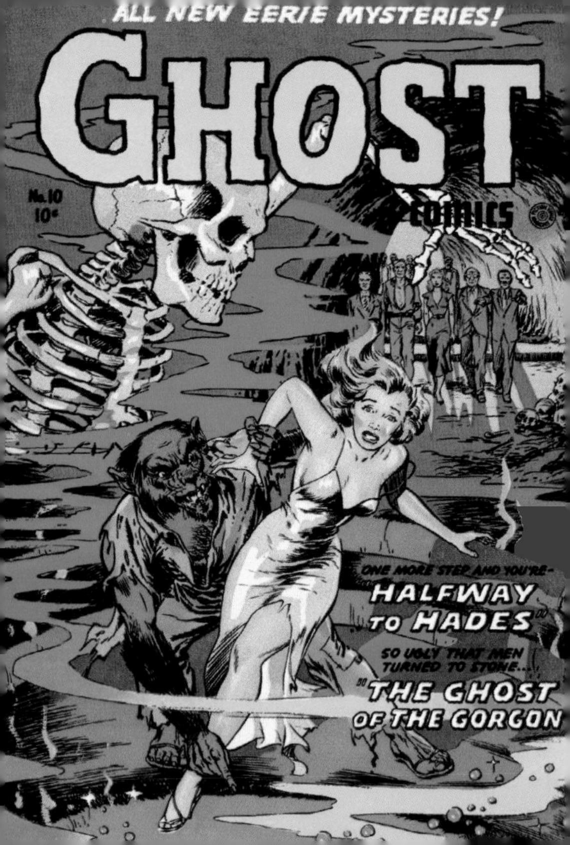
ALL NEW EERIE MYSTERIES!
GHOST
COMICS
No. 10
10¢
ONE MORE STEP AND YOU'RE-
"HALFWAY TO HADES"
SO UGLY THAT MEN TURNED TO STONE...
"THE GHOST OF THE GORGON"

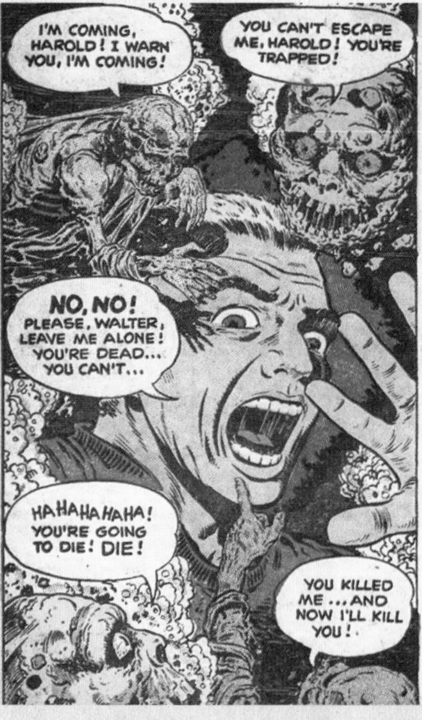
I'M COMING, HAROLD! I WARN YOU, I'M COMING!
YOU CAN'T ESCAPE ME, HAROLD! YOU'RE TRAPPED!
NO, NO! PLEASE, WALTER, LEAVE ME ALONE! YOU'RE DEAD... YOU CAN'T...
HAHAHAHAHAHA! YOU'RE GOING TO DIE! DIE!
YOU KILLED ME ... AND NOW I'LL KILL YOU!

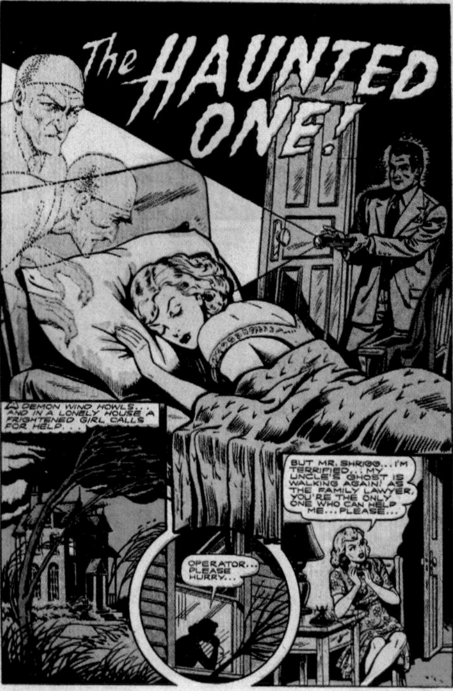
The HAUNTED ONE!
A DEMON WIND HOWLS... AND IN A LONELY HOUSE A FRIGHTENED GIRL CALLS FOR HELP...
OPERATOR... PLEASE HURRY...
BUT MR. SHRIGG... I'M TERRIFIED... MY UNCLE'S GHOST IS WALKING AGAIN! AS THE FAMILY LAWYER, YOU'RE THE ONLY ONE WHO CAN HELP ME... PLEASE...

THE Satchel

The alleyway was behind me as I came out into Parson Street. I looked down at the street lamp, looked at the man beneath lighting a cigarette, and gripped the handle of the black bag. He was the only one on the block.

I passed him. He exhaled a glob of smoke and took an ordinary look at me. I rounded the corner and came out on Damon Avenue, a small strip that was shouldered on both sides by ramshackle fences.

I crawled into the shadows and looked back. The man was coming in my direction. He inhaled on his cigarette and I saw his face in its pale glow. It was small but pudgy, with folds rippling through it.

He punched the air with a finger. "Hey, you!" he called.

Stepping back, I quickly sized up Damon Avenue. I gripped the bag tighter and ran. The ground churned beneath me and, for a split second, there was no ground. I landed flush in someone's back yard.

I made out the silhouette of a house before me which ended abruptly and, about eight feet away, I saw the dim outline of another house.

A shaft of light pounded into the darkness, accompanied by the dull rumbling of a window being opened. I looked up. Someone stuck his head out... "Who's there?"

A voice form behind the fence answered.

"It's him," it growled, "the man with the satchel."

I ran towards the blackness between the two houses, turned, and headed down a driveway. Gravel pebbles spilled behind me. The black bag swayed with every step.

Some stiff hedges snapped against my side and I entered them. Thorns cut my face as I came out on the other side. Turning around, I heard the staccato crunching of gravel, then the sharp retort of the pudgy man's voice. "Stop...!"

Suddenly, something sounding like a siren belted out. It was a woman's scream. She was directly in front of me, and I pushed her aside, running towards the end of the street.

I stopped, and slowly hoisted the satchel protectively in the nestle of my arm. The man with the pudgy face was coming down the street, walking slowly.

"Give me that bag," he said. I backed up, away from him, and wheeled. Another man was on the other side of me. I stopped. I looked at the pudgy-faced man again; he was nearer.

"You've got a bomb in that bag," he said. "The radio told us to be on the look-out for you."

Then, I was twisted around, and the second man hit me. I felt dizzy. He hit me again. I tumbled forward, face-downward.

Rolling over, I opened my eyes. The two men had the black bag opened. I managed to smile.

They looked down at me, dropped the bag, and ran. The black bag fell near me and my other head rolled out. I watched it as it halted by the curb.

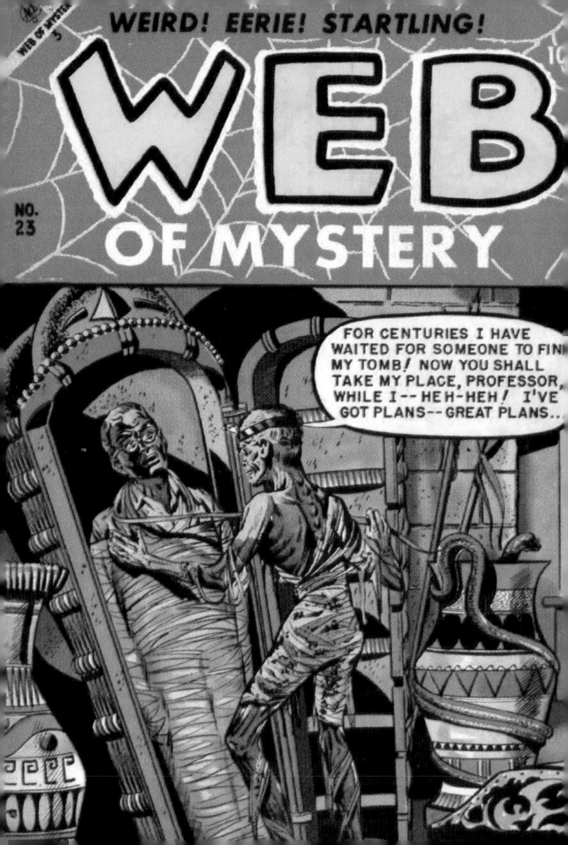
WEIRD! EERIE! STARTLING!
WEB
NO. 23
OF MYSTERY
FOR CENTURIES I HAVE WAITED FOR SOMEONE TO FIN MY TOMB! NOW YOU SHALL TAKE MY PLACE, PROFESSOR, WHILE I -- HEH-HEH! I'VE GOT PLANS -- GREAT PLANS..

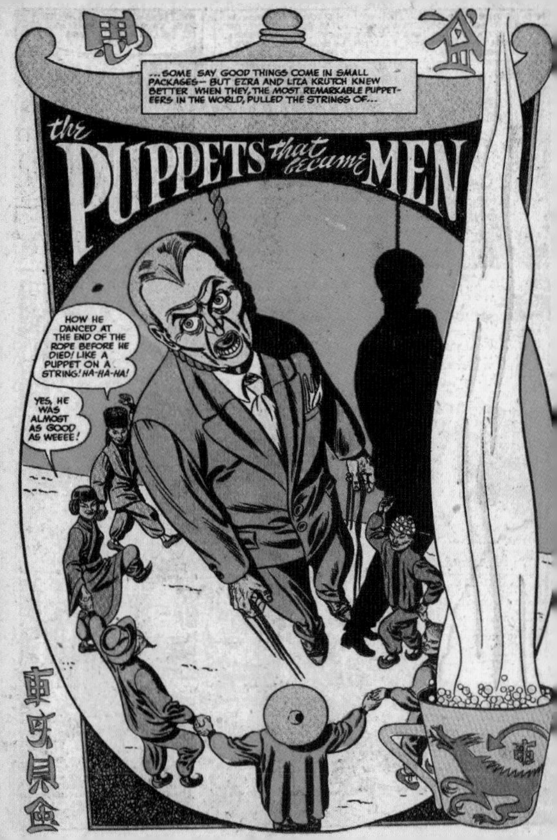
...SOME SAY GOOD THINGS COME IN SMALL PACKAGES-- BUT EZRA AND LIZA KRUTCH KNEW BETTER WHEN THEY, THE MOST REMARKABLE PUPPETEERS IN THE WORLD, PULLED THE STRINGS OF...
the PUPPETS that became MEN
HOW HE DANCED AT THE END OF THE ROPE BEFORE HE DIED! LIKE A PUPPET ON A STRING! HA-HA-HA!
YES, HE WAS ALMOST AS GOOD AS WEEEE!

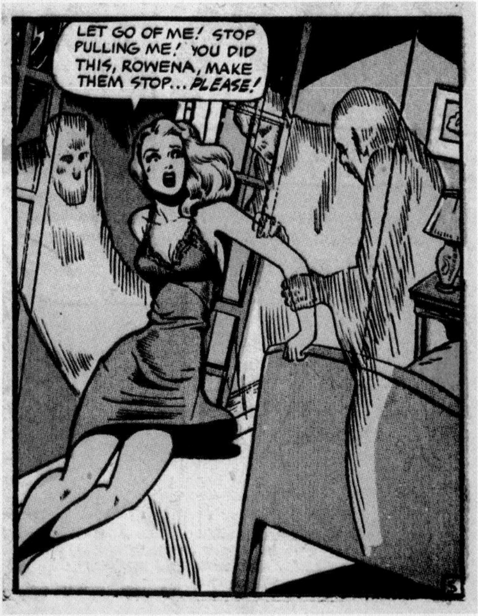
LET GO OF ME! STOP PULLING ME! YOU DID THIS, ROWENA, MAKE THEM STOP... PLEASE!

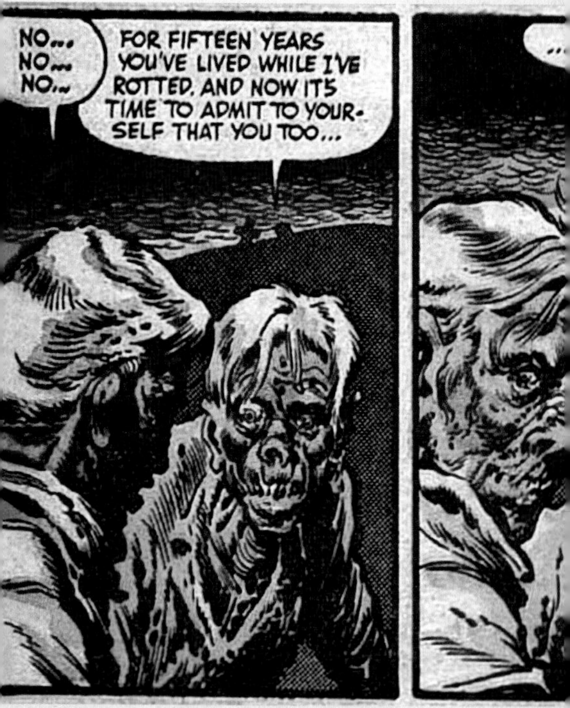
NO... NO... NO...
FOR FIFTEEN YEARS YOU'VE LIVED WHILE I'VE ROTTED, AND NOW IT'S TIME TO ADMIT TO YOURSELF THAT YOU TOO...

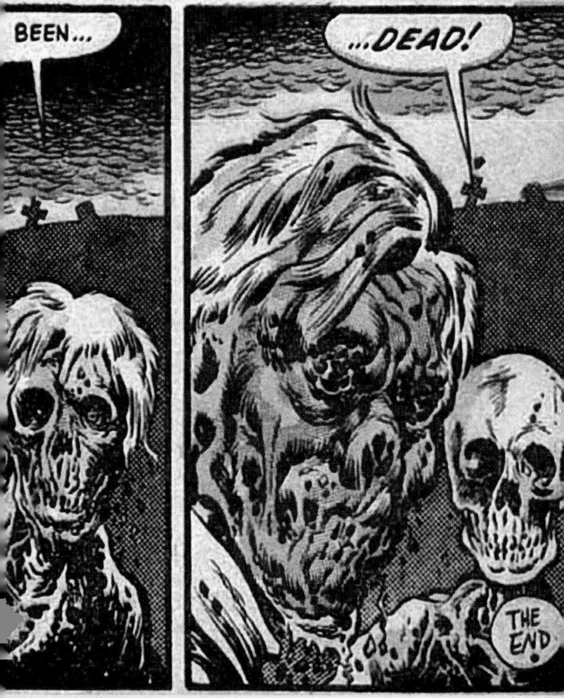
BEEN...
...DEAD!
THE END

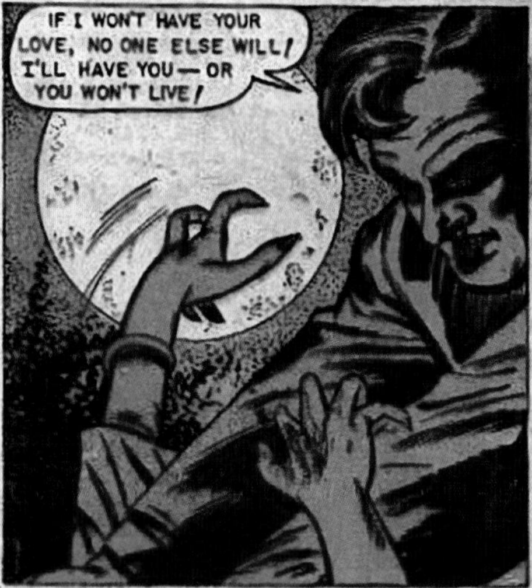
IF I WON'T HAVE YOUR LOVE, NO ONE ELSE WILL! I'LL HAVE YOU—OR YOU WON'T LIVE!

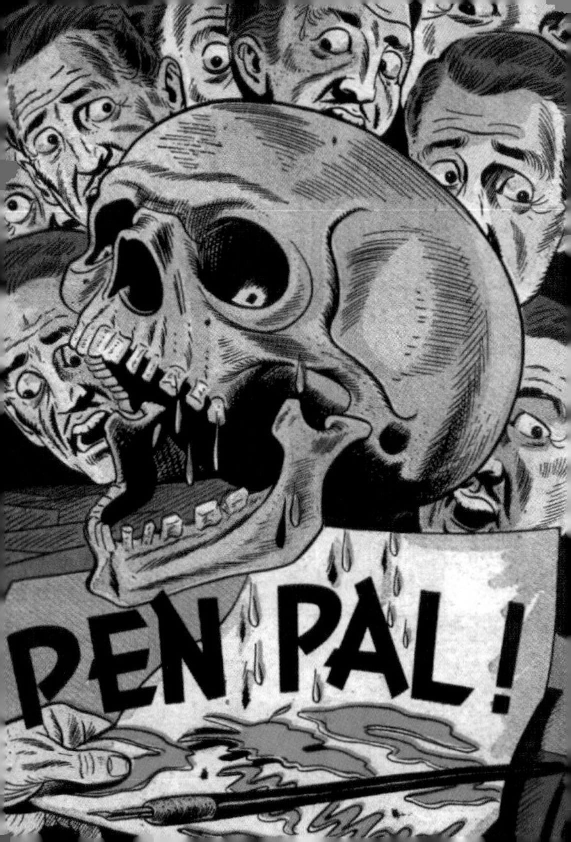
PEN PAL!

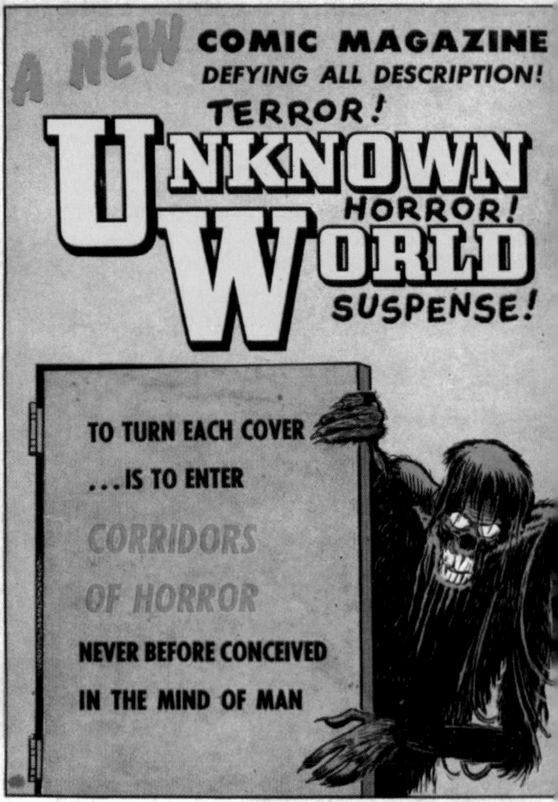
A NEW
COMIC MAGAZINE
DEFYING ALL DESCRIPTION!
TERROR!
UNKNOWN
HORROR!
WORLD
SUSPENSE!
TO TURN EACH COVER
...IS TO ENTER
CORRIDORS
OF HORROR
NEVER BEFORE CONCEIVED
IN THE MIND OF MAN

10¢ ON SALE AT YOUR FAVORITE NEWSSTAND 10¢

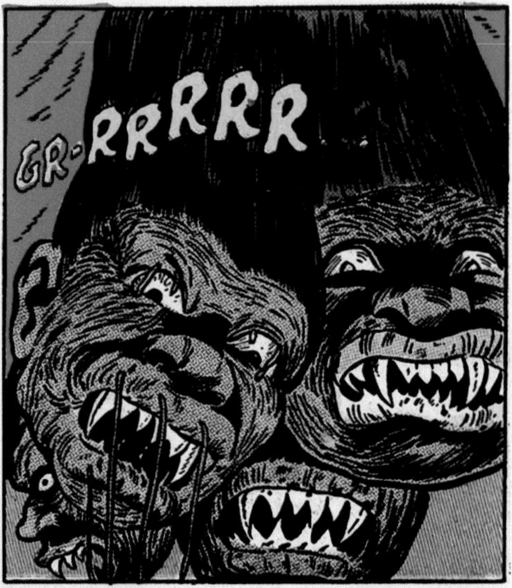
GR-RRRRR...

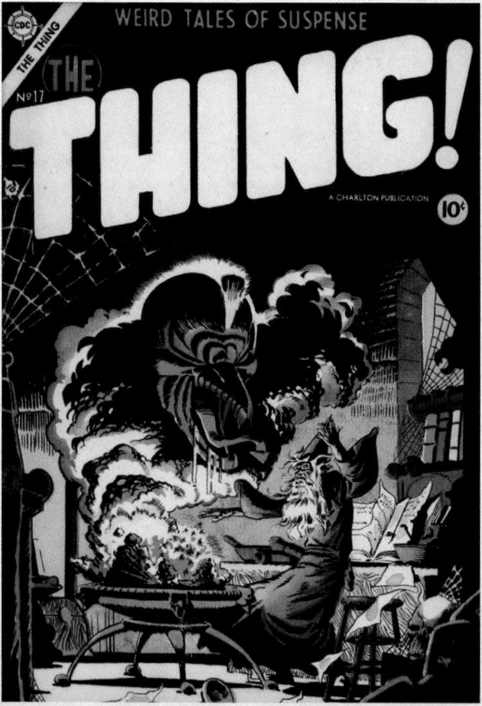

CDC
THE THING
WEIRD TALES OF SUSPENSE
THE THING!
Nº17
A CHARLTON PUBLICATION
10¢

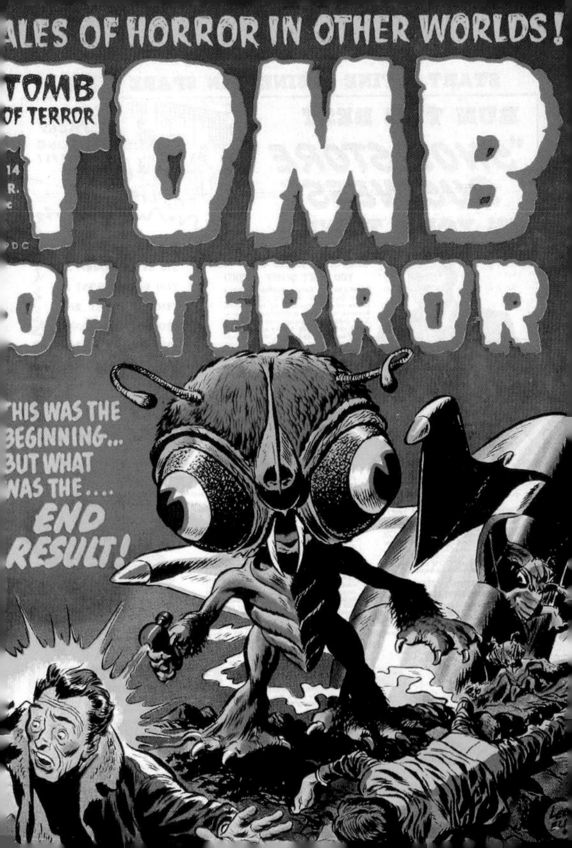
ALES OF HORROR IN OTHER WORLDS!
TOMB OF TERROR
TOMB OF TERROR
HIS WAS THE
EGINNING...
UT WHAT
VAS THE....
END
RESULT!

YOU CROUCH AGAINST THE STINKING MOIST ALLEY WALL, GERALD WILLIA
...YOUR BREATHE STICKS IN YOUR THROAT... AND YOUR EYES BULGE WIT
FEAR... FOR FACING YOU, IS THE DREADED FIGURE WHO'S ON A KILLING
SPREE THAT IS COMPARABLE ONLY TO THAT OF...

JACK the RIPPER

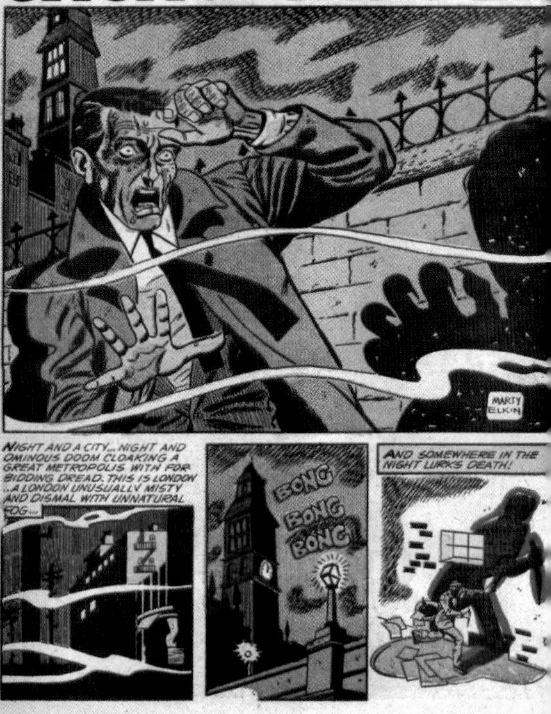
MARTY ELKIN
NIGHT AND A CITY... NIGHT AND OMINOUS DOOM CLOAKING A GREAT METROPOLIS WITH FOR BIDDING DREAD. THIS IS LONDON ...A LONDON UNUSUALLY MISTY AND DISMAL WITH UNNATURAL FOG...
BONG
BONG
BONG!
AND SOMEWHERE IN THE NIGHT LURKS DEATH!

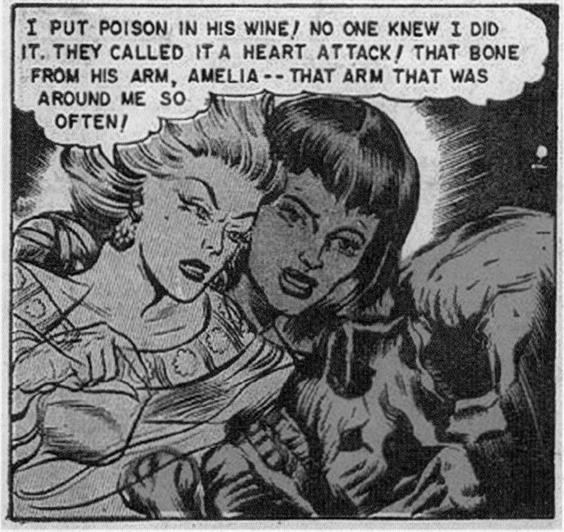
I PUT POISON IN HIS WINE! NO ONE KNEW I DID IT. THEY CALLED IT A HEART ATTACK! THAT BONE FROM HIS ARM, AMELIA -- THAT ARM THAT WAS AROUND ME SO OFTEN!

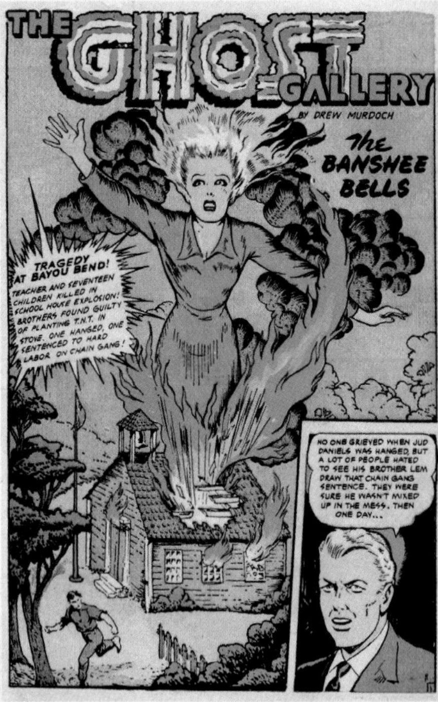
THE GHOST GALLERY
BY DREW MURDOCH
The BANSHEE BELLS
TRAGEDY AT BAYOU BEND! TEACHER AND SEVENTEEN CHILDREN KILLED IN SCHOOL HOUSE EXPLOSION! BROTHERS FOUND GUILTY OF PLANTING T.N.T. IN STOVE. ONE HANGED, ONE SENTENCED TO HARD LABOR ON CHAIN GANG!
NO ONE GRIEVED WHEN JUD DANIELS WAS HANGED, BUT A LOT OF PEOPLE HATED TO SEE HIS BROTHER LEM DRAW THAT CHAIN GANG SENTENCE. THEY WERE SURE HE WASN'T MIXED UP IN THE MESS. THEN ONE DAY...

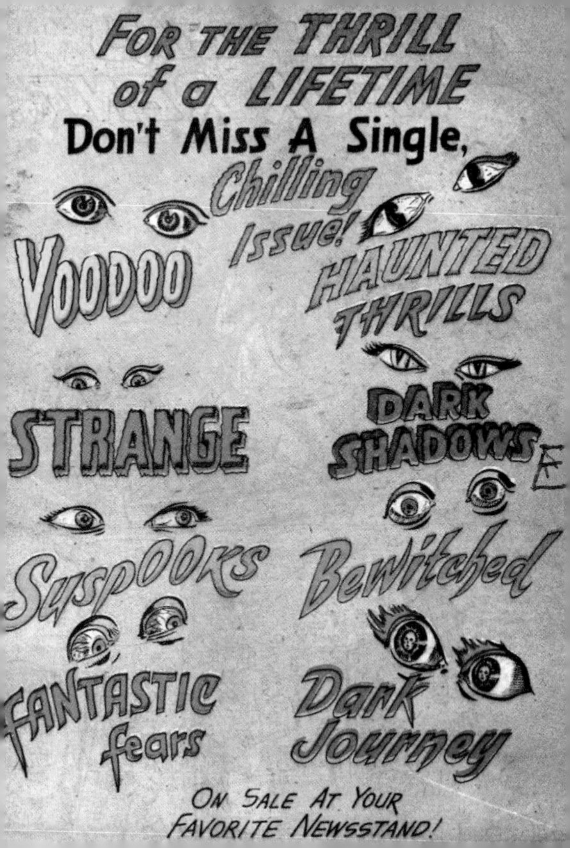

FOR THE THRILL
of a LIFETIME
Don't Miss A Single,
Chilling
Issue!
VOODOO
HAUNTED
THRILLS
STRANGE
DARK
SHADOWS
SUSPOOKS
Bewitched
FANTASTIC
fears
Dark
Journey
ON SALE AT YOUR
FAVORITE NEWSSTAND!

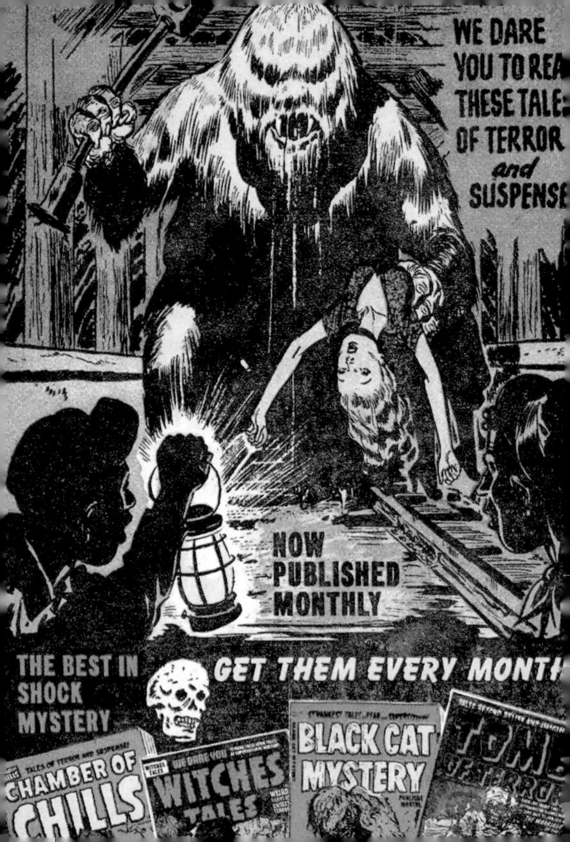
WE DARE
YOU TO REA
THESE TALE
OF TERROR
and
SUSPENSE
NOW
PUBLISHED
MONTHLY
THE BEST IN
SHOCK
MYSTERY
GET THEM EVERY MONTH
TALES OF TERROR AND SUSPENSE!
CHAMBER OF
CHILLS
WE DARE YOU
WITCHES
TALES
BLACK CAT
MYSTERY

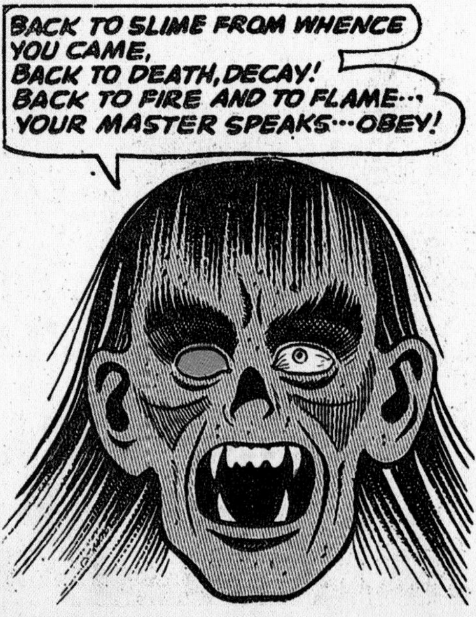
BACK TO SLIME FROM WHENCE
YOU CAME,
BACK TO DEATH, DECAY!
BACK TO FIRE AND TO FLAME...
YOUR MASTER SPEAKS...OBEY!

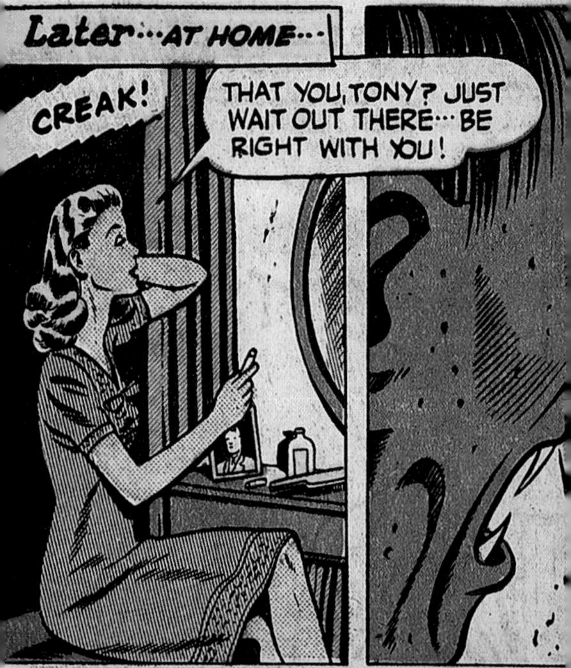
Later...AT HOME...
CREAK!
THAT YOU, TONY? JUST WAIT OUT THERE... BE RIGHT WITH YOU!

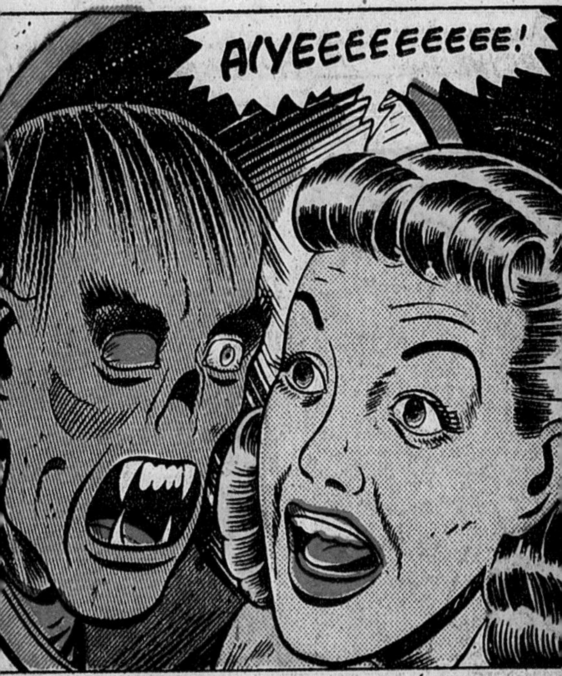
AIYEEEEEEEEEE!

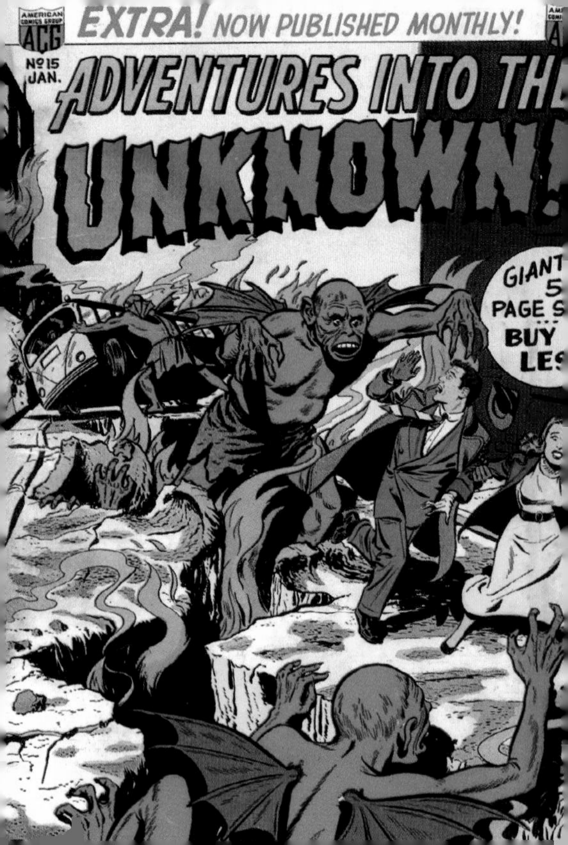

AMERICAN COMICS GROUP
ACG
EXTRA! NOW PUBLISHED MONTHLY!
No 15
JAN.
ADVENTURES INTO TH
UNKNOWN!
GIANT 5 PAGE S... BUY LES

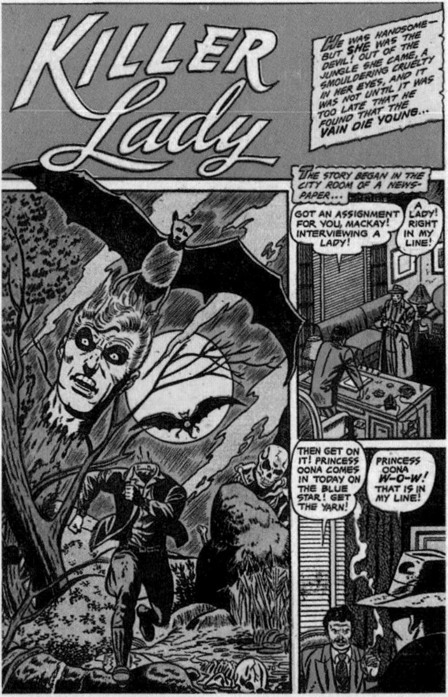
KILLER Lady
HE WAS HANDSOME—BUT SHE WAS THE DEVIL! OUT OF THE JUNGLE SHE CAME, A SMOULDERING CRUELTY IN HER EYES, AND IT WAS NOT UNTIL IT WAS TOO LATE THAT HE FOUND THAT THE VAIN DIE YOUNG...
THE STORY BEGAN IN THE CITY ROOM OF A NEWSPAPER...
GOT AN ASSIGNMENT FOR YOU, MACKAY! INTERVIEWING A LADY!
A LADY! RIGHT IN MY LINE!
THEN GET ON IT! PRINCESS OONA COMES IN TODAY ON THE BLUE STAR! GET THE YARN!
PRINCESS OONA W-O-W! THAT IS IN MY LINE!

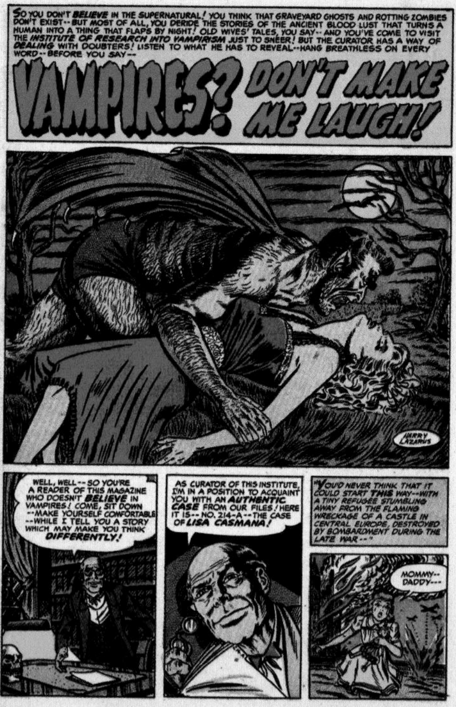
SO YOU DON'T BELIEVE IN THE SUPERNATURAL! YOU THINK THAT GRAVEYARD GHOSTS AND ROTTING ZOMBIES DON'T EXIST--BUT MOST OF ALL, YOU DERIDE THE STORIES OF THE ANCIENT BLOOD LUST THAT TURNS A HUMAN INTO A THING THAT FLAPS BY NIGHT! OLD WIVES' TALES, YOU SAY--AND YOU'VE COME TO VISIT THE INSTITUTE OF RESEARCH INTO VAMPIRISM JUST TO SNEER! BUT THE CURATOR HAS A WAY OF DEALING WITH DOUBTERS! LISTEN TO WHAT HE HAS TO REVEAL--HANG BREATHLESS ON EVERY WORD--BEFORE YOU SAY--
VAMPIRES? DON'T MAKE ME LAUGH!
HARRY LAZARUS
WELL, WELL--SO YOU'RE A READER OF THIS MAGAZINE WHO DOESN'T BELIEVE IN VAMPIRES! COME, SIT DOWN--MAKE YOURSELF COMFORTABLE--WHILE I TELL YOU A STORY WHICH MAY MAKE YOU THINK DIFFERENTLY!
AS CURATOR OF THIS INSTITUTE, I'M IN A POSITION TO ACQUAINT YOU WITH AN AUTHENTIC CASE FROM OUR FILES! HERE IT IS--NO. 214-A--THE CASE OF LISA CASMANA!
"YOU'D NEVER THINK THAT IT COULD START THIS WAY--WITH A TINY REFUGEE STUMBLING AWAY FROM THE FLAMING WRECKAGE OF A CASTLE IN CENTRAL EUROPE, DESTROYED BY BOMBARDMENT DURING THE LATE WAR--"
MOMMY--DADDY---

THE CELLAR OF BLOOD!

The world believes that Heinrich Himmler killed himself when he was finally captured. But the Army of Occupation Intelligence has heard a different story. We heard that the man who died was a double, and that Himmler actually had suicided in hiding and was secretly buried by his storm troop comrades. We had been searching for his burial place for some time—to learn the facts, for Himmler had been the foulest murderer in the world's history—six million had been the number of his innocent victims.

A captain, I had been attracted by a strange story told at one of our hospitals. Several men had been placed under restraint there. They had all been on guard duty near the old castle Aldenweir. Each had been found raving crazy in the morning . . . and the name of Himmler had been mentioned in their ravings.

After listening to some of them I took a jeep and drove out to that partly ruined castle. The sun was setting. It was ancient, gloomy, forbidding. Darkness was falling as I entered, and my search-light barely illuminated a small area of the damp ruins. Groping back doorways . . . slimy worn steps . . . the whirr of bats was all about me! I heard a strange sound from below.

I descended the stairs that led down into the dungeon cellar. They twisted eerily and were treacherously steep. At the bottom, I found myself treading in something wet. I flashed my light down and saw that the floor of the old basement was covered with something sticky and moist. I heard the noise again; it seemed like a choking sort of screaming. A faint reddish light shone.

Towards it I made my way slowly, my feet sucking deeper into the muck of the floor. An odor as of a butcher shop assailed my nostrils. I saw something coming towards me, stopped, called. There was no answer, only a sickly dripping sound and the choking. Then, around a pillar, it came into view.

It was a man, swollen, bloated, ten feet tall! It was greenish and monstrous. It was tailed and horned and scaly. Its face, distorted though it was, was that of the unspeakable Himmler! From every pore, from fingers and toes and torso, blood was dripping! It was blood, I realized, that covered the floor. Blood that flowed from this monster! The horror moved forwards towards me, groping, dripping, gurgling!

I stood there, transfixed with terror. I screamed, then turned and fought my way out of that castle, my feet slipping and sliding in a sea of gore.

Next day I recovered enough to call in a crew of G.I. engineers. They dug in that basement, covered with dried red scum, and they turned up the body of a man—of Heinrich Himmler. He had been buried there. They burned that body in a bonfire outside the castle.

What I had seen was the ghost of the greatest fiend that had ever lived in all the ten thousand tortured years of history. Dead though he was, he was doomed to wallow in that ocean of blood he had caused to flow. Burned, his ashes scattered, Himmler's ghost would walk no more!

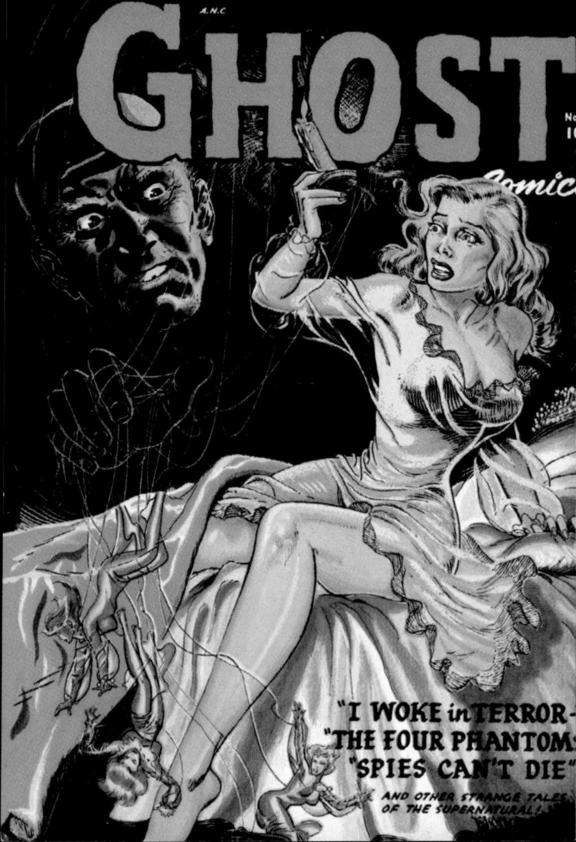

A.N.C
GHOST
Comics
"I WOKE in TERROR-
"THE FOUR PHANTOM
"SPIES CAN'T DIE"
AND OTHER STRANGE TALES OF THE SUPERNATURAL!

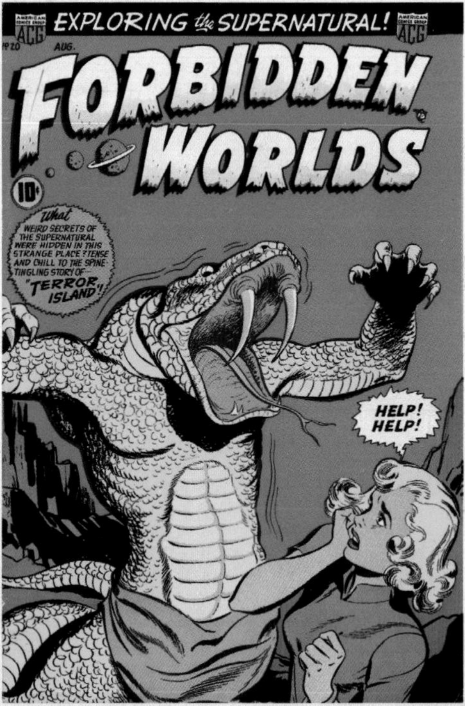

EXPLORING the SUPERNATURAL!
ACG
No 20
AUG.
FORBIDDEN WORLDS
10¢
What WEIRD SECRETS OF THE SUPERNATURAL WERE HIDDEN IN THIS STRANGE PLACE? TENSE AND CHILL TO THE SPINE-TINGLING STORY OF— "TERROR ISLAND"!
HELP! HELP!

MEANWHILE, TONY ISN'T GIVING UP! DESPERATELY HUNTING FOR SOME SIGN OF THE LIVING GHOST'S TRAIL, HE SEARCHES THE SCENE OF THE LAST MURDER! AND SUDDENLY HE SEES···
H-HOLY HANNAH! WHAT···
8.

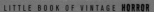

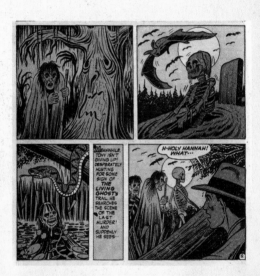

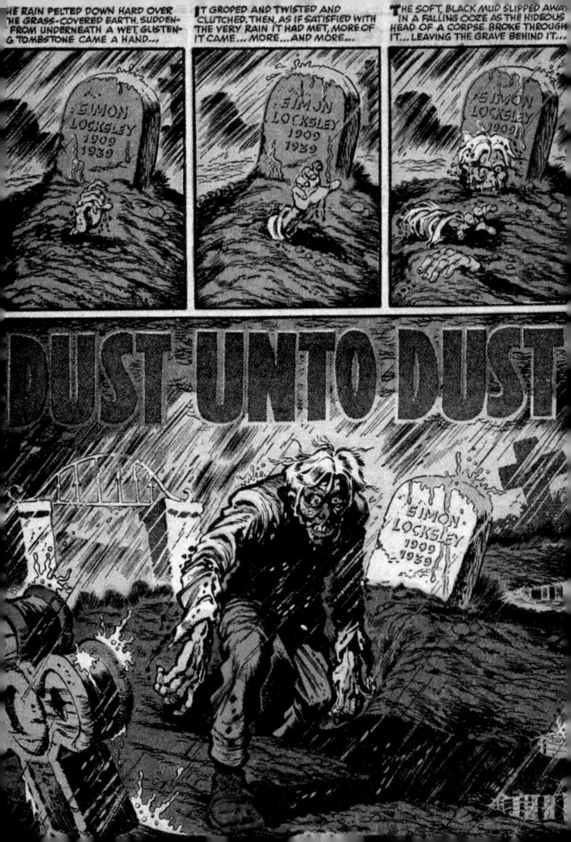
HE RAIN PELTED DOWN HARD OVER HE GRASS-COVERED EARTH. SUDDEN- FROM UNDERNEATH A WET, GLISTEN- G TOMBSTONE CAME A HAND...
SIMON LOCKSLEY 1909 1939
IT GROPED AND TWISTED AND CLUTCHED. THEN, AS IF SATISFIED WITH THE VERY RAIN IT HAD MET, MORE OF IT CAME... MORE... AND MORE...
SIMON LOCKSLEY 1909 1939
THE SOFT, BLACK MUD SLIPPED AWAY IN A FALLING OOZE AS THE HIDEOUS HEAD OF A CORPSE BROKE THROUGH IT... LEAVING THE GRAVE BEHIND IT...
SIMON LOCKSLEY 1909
DUST UNTO DUST
SIMON LOCKSLEY 1909 1939

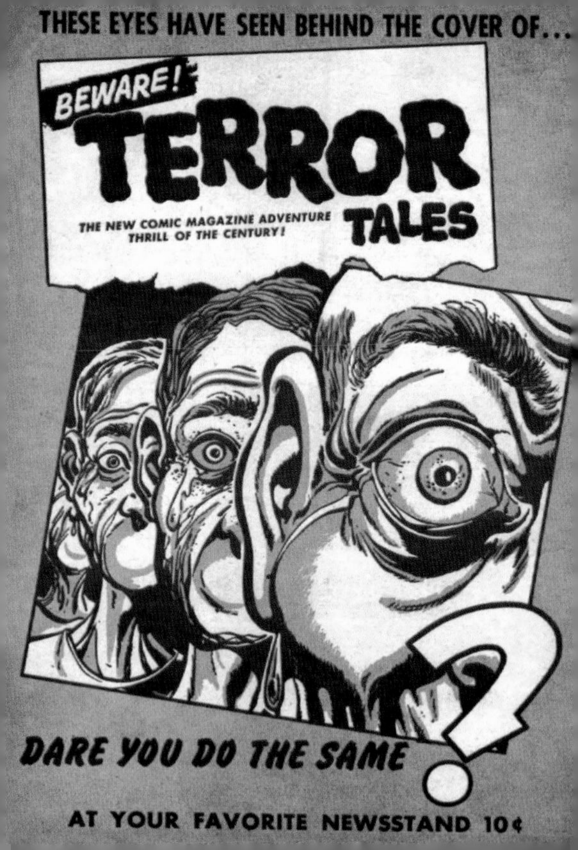
THESE EYES HAVE SEEN BEHIND THE COVER OF...
BEWARE!
TERROR TALES
THE NEW COMIC MAGAZINE ADVENTURE THRILL OF THE CENTURY!
DARE YOU DO THE SAME?
AT YOUR FAVORITE NEWSSTAND 10¢

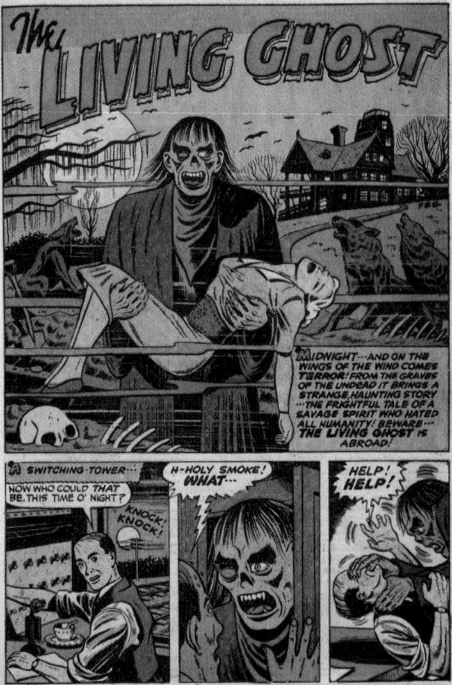
The LIVING GHOST
MIDNIGHT...AND ON THE WINGS OF THE WIND COMES TERROR! FROM THE GRAVES OF THE UNDEAD IT BRINGS A STRANGE, HAUNTING STORY ...THE FRIGHTFUL TALE OF A SAVAGE SPIRIT WHO HATED ALL HUMANITY! BEWARE... THE LIVING GHOST IS ABROAD!
A SWITCHING TOWER...
NOW WHO COULD THAT BE, THIS TIME O' NIGHT?
KNOCK! KNOCK!
H-HOLY SMOKE! WHAT...
HELP! HELP!

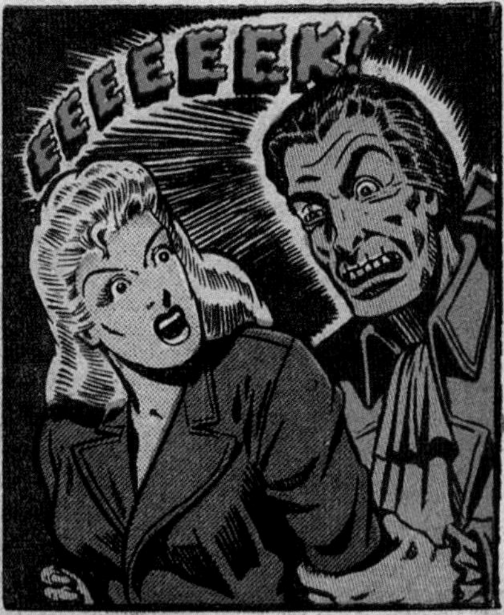
EEEEEEK!

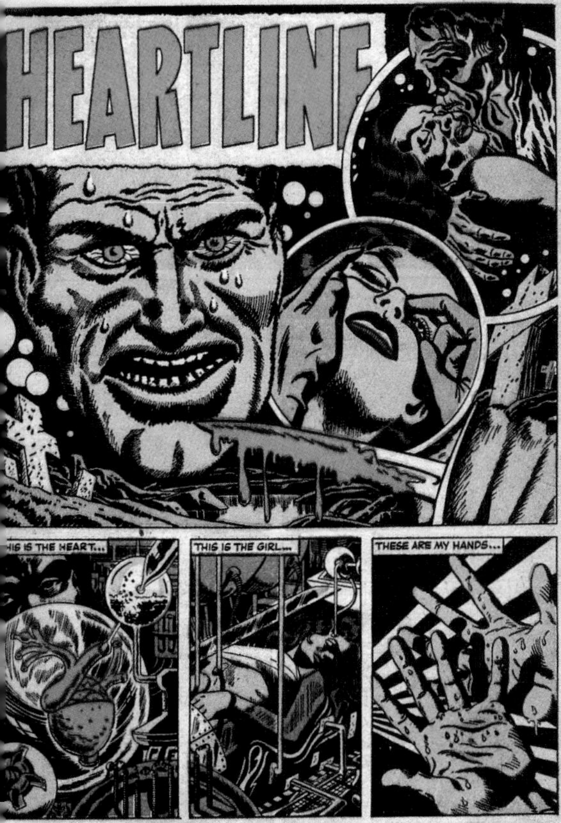
HEARTLINE
THIS IS THE HEART...
THIS IS THE GIRL...
THESE ARE MY HANDS...

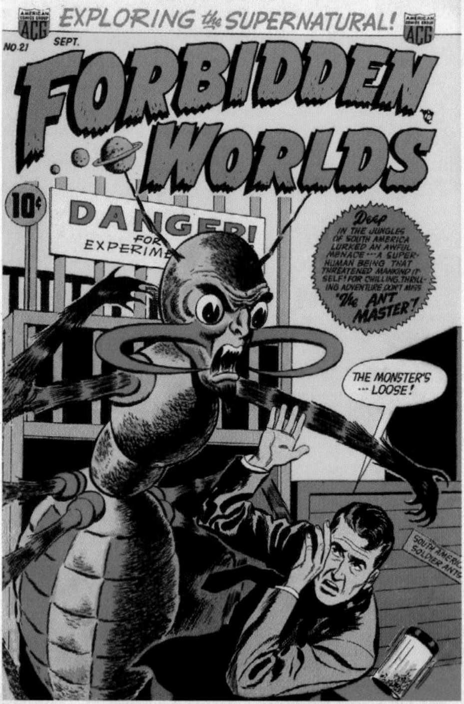
EXPLORING the SUPERNATURAL!
ACG
ACG
NO.21
SEPT.
FORBIDDEN WORLDS
10¢
DANGER!
FOR
EXPERIME
Deep IN THE JUNGLES OF SOUTH AMERICA LURKED AN AWFUL MENACE --- A SUPER-HUMAN BEING THAT THREATENED MANKIND IT-SELF! FOR CHILLING, THRILL-ING ADVENTURE DON'T MISS "The ANT MASTER"!
THE MONSTER'S --- LOOSE!
SOUTH AMERIC
SOLDIER ANTS

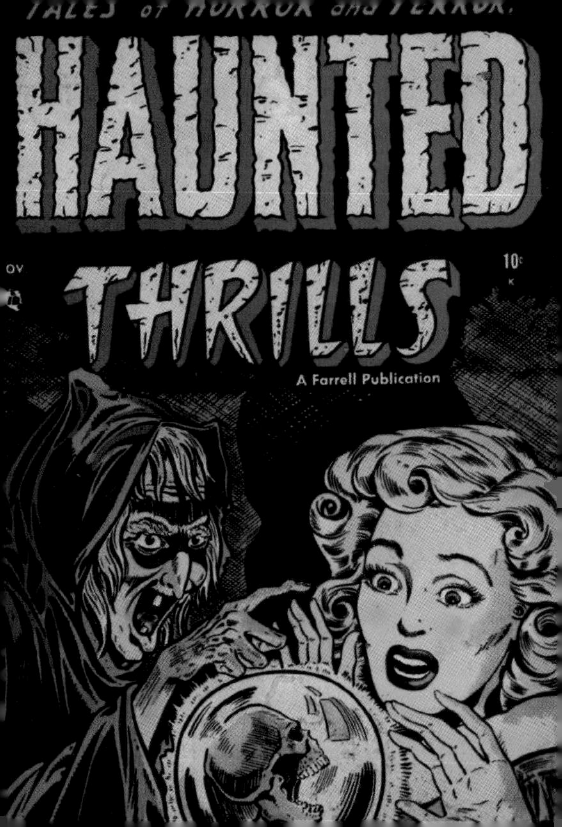
TALES of HORROR and TERROR
HAUNTED
THRILLS
10¢
A Farrell Publication

HOTEL HORROR

AFTER THREE WEEKS on a special assignment, Detective Joe Hollis had discovered nothing. It was true that everything about the gloomy old place was odd, even creepy, but he couldn't put his finger on anything specific.

Almost twenty people had disappeared during the past year whose last address had been this little hotel in the heart of midtown Manhattan. He had been ordered to take up residence there incognito, and to get to the bottom of the strange mystery.

Almost immediately he noticed that an extraordinary number of orientals checked in and out. The hotel owners themselves were from India, quite peculiar people, not given to friendly conversation.

But the person who interested him most was the girl in the room next to his, a bewitchingly beautiful young oriental with dark, mysterious eyes and a strangely remote manner.

Many times he had tried to strike up an acquaintance with her, but each time she had firmly put him in his place. What astonished him most was that the girl was often in her room for days on end without ever leaving, and as far as he could tell no food of any kind was sent up to her.

Her few visitors were usually Indians like herself, but occasionally there were other guests. Not long before a queer thought had struck him. Offhand, it seemed that more people entered her room than *left* it! He couldn't be sure; perhaps there was another exit to the room. But he was determined to find out. Somehow he felt that she was in some way connected with the ghastly mystery, incredible as that seemed.

He waited patiently for the right time. Then, watching her leave the hotel in the early evening, and since nobody was in the corridors, he let himself into her room with a passkey.

It was an amazing room, entirely bare except for a thick layer of *sand* strewn across the floor and a large potted tree in the center, whose thick branches were flattened against the ceiling. That was all, except for a complete female wardrobe in the closet.

He scratched his head in astonishment as an incredible idea came to him. "That tree," he thought. "What's it for? And the sand on the floor . . . you'd almost think a *snake* was living in this room!"

At that moment his head shot round, for the doorhandle had turned. Instantly his hand darted to his gun holster. The beautiful girl was already inside, her delicate lips curled in an expression of rage.

"Leave this room!" she hissed. "At once!"

"Not until I find out what's going on, sister," he snapped back. "What's all this about? How come there's no regular furniture in here, no bed, no . . . "

The words died in his throat as a shock of terror swept over him. For as he stood petrified, the girl was *changing* . . . into a full-sized *cobra!*

He never had a chance to fire his gun, for the serpent struck with lightning speed, its leathery coils choking off his breath, making the room spin before his eyes.

"Couldn't you guess?" a weird female voice hissed into his ear. "I *sleep* in that tree . . . where am I like *this!* Many of us in this hotel belong to an ancient Indian cult, which you westerners call mere superstition! Thus, you make our work easy!"

The young detective's knees gave way, and everything grew swiftly darker. He could barely hear her now as the voice became little more than a serpent's hiss.

"How could the police suspect the truth of what goes on in this hotel," he heard as from far away, "when our victims never leave behind remains?"

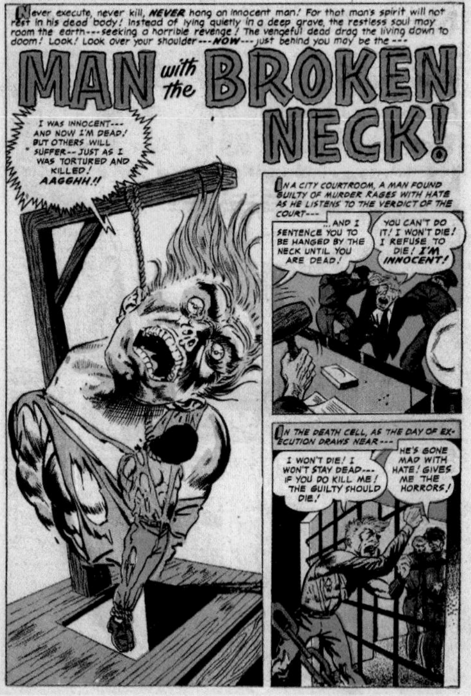
Never execute, never kill, NEVER hang an innocent man! For that man's spirit will not rest in his dead body! Instead of lying quietly in a deep grave, the restless soul may roam the earth---seeking a horrible revenge! The vengeful dead drag the living down to doom! Look! Look over your shoulder---NOW---just behind you may be the ---
MAN with the BROKEN NECK!
I WAS INNOCENT--- AND NOW I'M DEAD! BUT OTHERS WILL SUFFER-- JUST AS I WAS TORTURED AND KILLED! AAGGHH!!
IN A CITY COURTROOM, A MAN FOUND GUILTY OF MURDER RAGES WITH HATE AS HE LISTENS TO THE VERDICT OF THE COURT---
... AND I SENTENCE YOU TO BE HANGED BY THE NECK UNTIL YOU ARE DEAD!
YOU CAN'T DO IT! I WON'T DIE! I REFUSE TO DIE! I'M INNOCENT!
IN THE DEATH CELL, AS THE DAY OF EXECUTION DRAWS NEAR---
I WON'T DIE! I WON'T STAY DEAD--- IF YOU DO KILL ME! THE GUILTY SHOULD DIE!
HE'S GONE MAD WITH HATE! GIVES ME THE HORRORS!

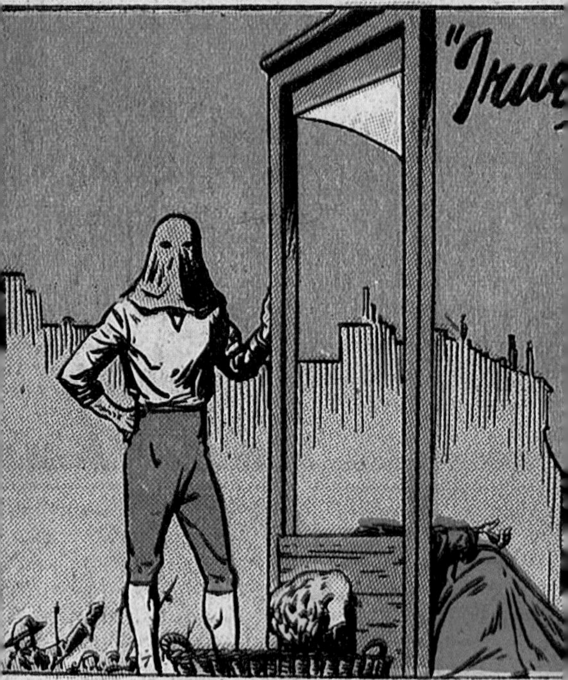

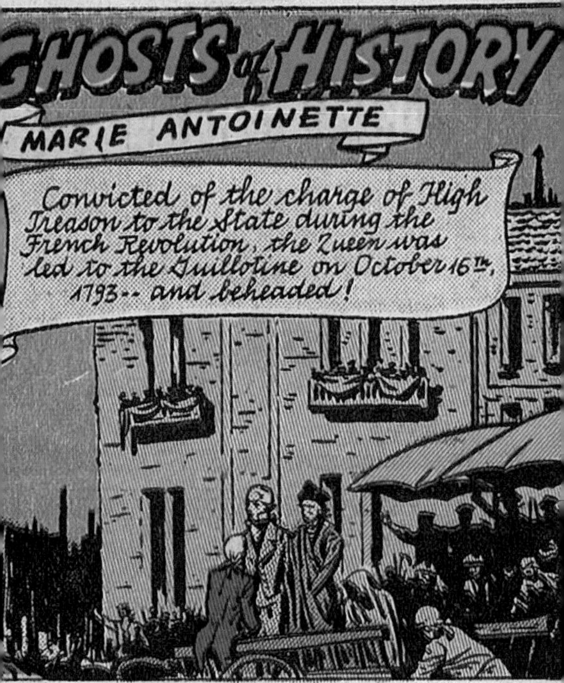
GHOSTS of HISTORY
MARIE ANTOINETTE
Convicted of the charge of High Treason to the State during the French Revolution, the Queen was led to the Guillotine on October 16th, 1793 -- and beheaded!

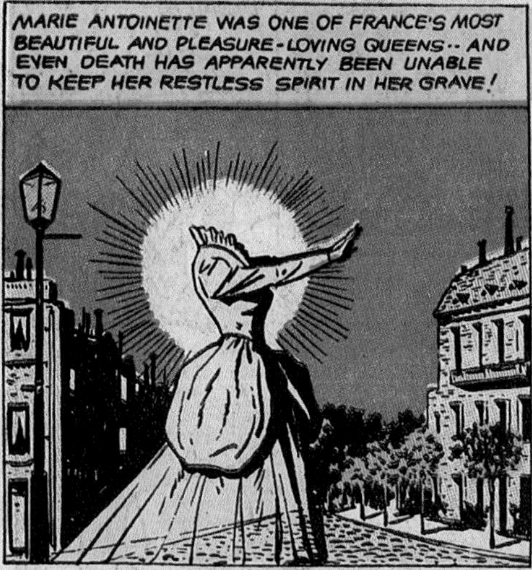
MARIE ANTOINETTE WAS ONE OF FRANCE'S MOST BEAUTIFUL AND PLEASURE-LOVING QUEENS-- AND EVEN DEATH HAS APPARENTLY BEEN UNABLE TO KEEP HER RESTLESS SPIRIT IN HER GRAVE!

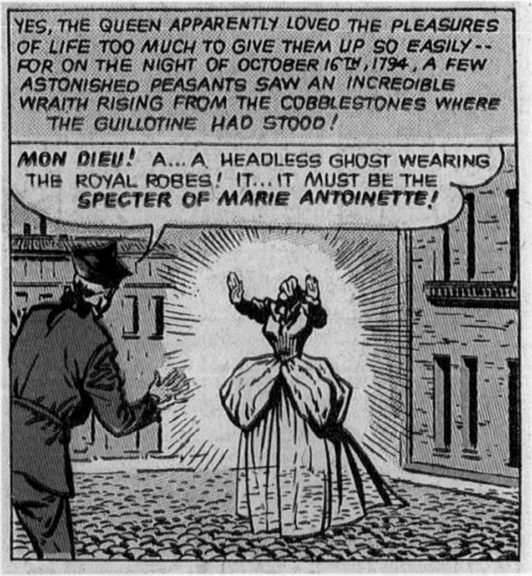
YES, THE QUEEN APPARENTLY LOVED THE PLEASURES OF LIFE TOO MUCH TO GIVE THEM UP SO EASILY -- FOR ON THE NIGHT OF OCTOBER 16TH, 1794, A FEW ASTONISHED PEASANTS SAW AN INCREDIBLE WRAITH RISING FROM THE COBBLESTONES WHERE THE GUILLOTINE HAD STOOD!
MON DIEU! A... A HEADLESS GHOST WEARING THE ROYAL ROBES! IT... IT MUST BE THE SPECTER OF MARIE ANTOINETTE!

EACH YEAR, IT IS SAID, THE GHOST OF MARIE ANTOINETTE MATERIALIZES ON THE ANNIVERSARY OF HER EXECUTION TO WALK THE STREETS FOR A FEW BRIEF HOURS, HER HANDS STRETCHED BEFORE HER AS IF TO FEEL THE WAY FOR HER SIGHTLESS BODY!

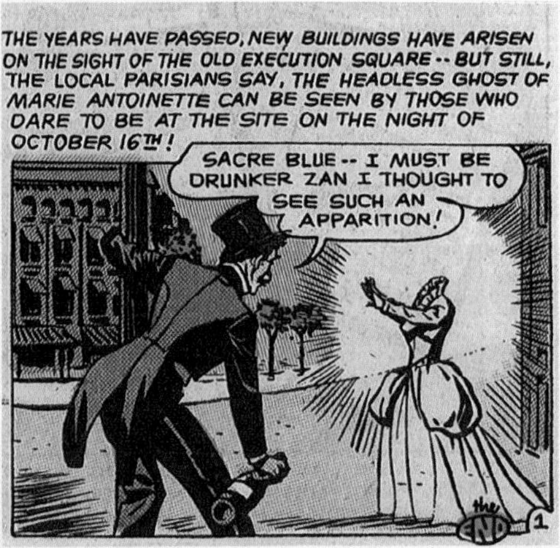
THE YEARS HAVE PASSED, NEW BUILDINGS HAVE ARISEN ON THE SIGHT OF THE OLD EXECUTION SQUARE -- BUT STILL, THE LOCAL PARISIANS SAY, THE HEADLESS GHOST OF MARIE ANTOINETTE CAN BE SEEN BY THOSE WHO DARE TO BE AT THE SITE ON THE NIGHT OF OCTOBER 16TH!
SACRE BLUE -- I MUST BE DRUNKER ZAN I THOUGHT TO SEE SUCH AN APPARITION!
the END

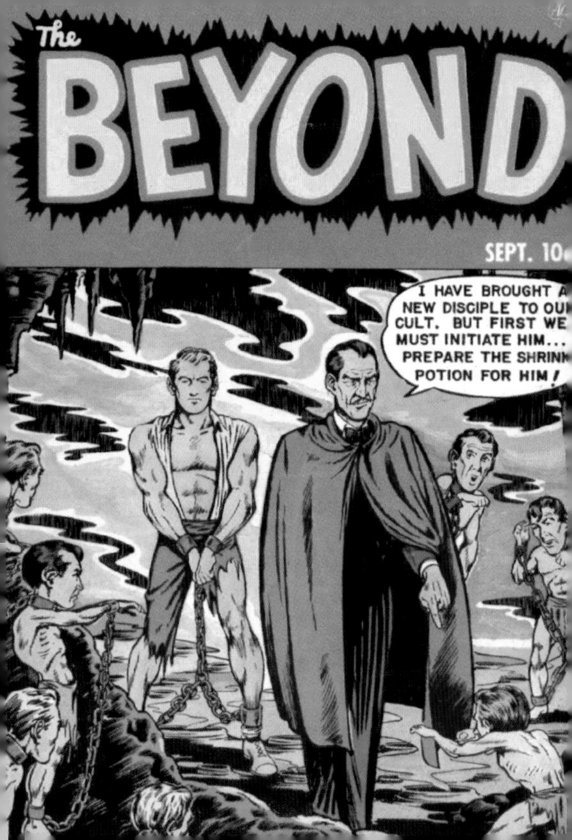

The
BEYOND
SEPT. 10¢
I HAVE BROUGHT A NEW DISCIPLE TO OUR CULT. BUT FIRST WE MUST INITIATE HIM... PREPARE THE SHRINK POTION FOR HIM!

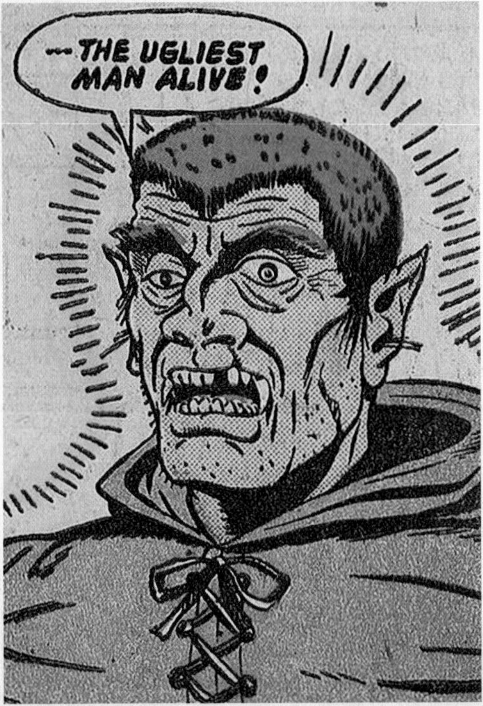
---THE UGLIEST MAN ALIVE!

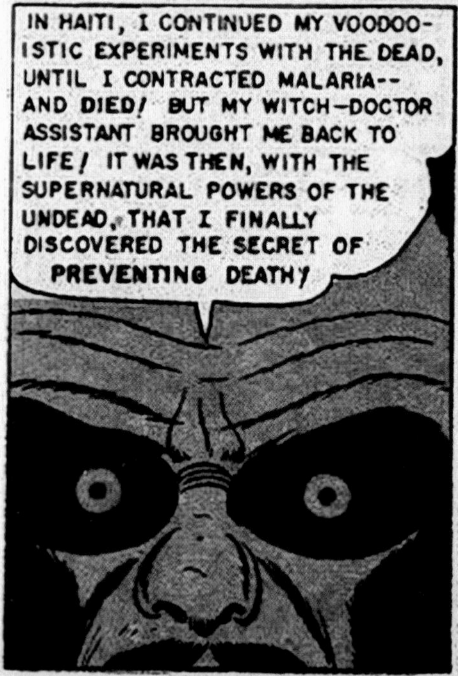
IN HAITI, I CONTINUED MY VOODOO-ISTIC EXPERIMENTS WITH THE DEAD, UNTIL I CONTRACTED MALARIA-- AND DIED! BUT MY WITCH-DOCTOR ASSISTANT BROUGHT ME BACK TO LIFE! IT WAS THEN, WITH THE SUPERNATURAL POWERS OF THE UNDEAD, THAT I FINALLY DISCOVERED THE SECRET OF PREVENTING DEATH!

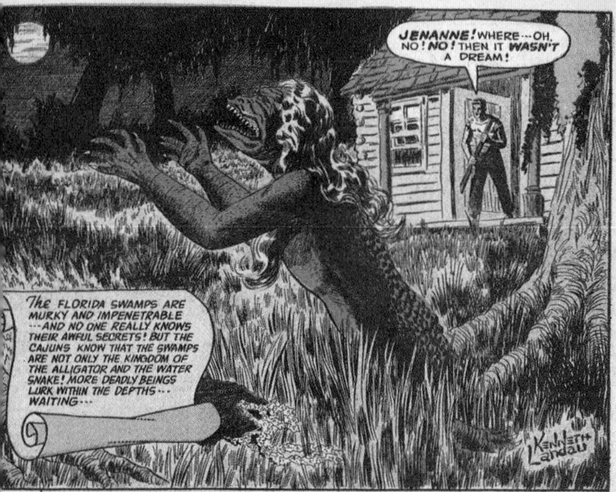
JENANNE! WHERE---OH, NO! NO! THEN IT WASN'T A DREAM!
The FLORIDA SWAMPS ARE MURKY AND IMPENETRABLE ---AND NO ONE REALLY KNOWS THEIR AWFUL SECRETS! BUT THE CAJUNS KNOW THAT THE SWAMPS ARE NOT ONLY THE KINGDOM OF THE ALLIGATOR AND THE WATER SNAKE! MORE DEADLY BEINGS LURK WITHIN THE DEPTHS--- WAITING---
KENNETH LANDAU

BRIDE of the SWAMP

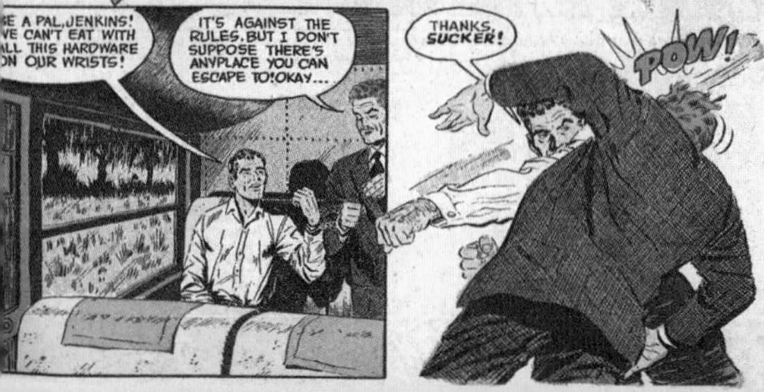
E A PAL, JENKINS! VE CAN'T EAT WITH LL THIS HARDWARE ON OUR WRISTS!
IT'S AGAINST THE RULES, BUT I DON'T SUPPOSE THERE'S ANYPLACE YOU CAN ESCAPE TO! OKAY...
THANKS, SUCKER!
POW!

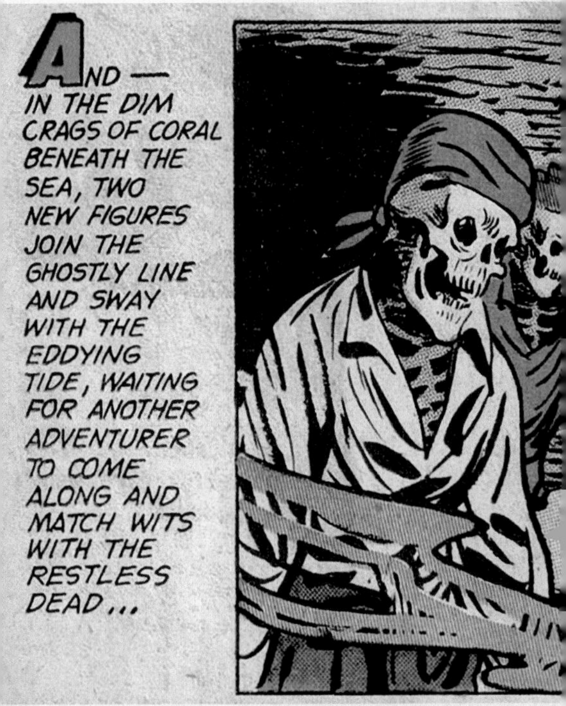
AND — IN THE DIM CRAGS OF CORAL BENEATH THE SEA, TWO NEW FIGURES JOIN THE GHOSTLY LINE AND SWAY WITH THE EDDYING TIDE, WAITING FOR ANOTHER ADVENTURER TO COME ALONG AND MATCH WITS WITH THE RESTLESS DEAD...

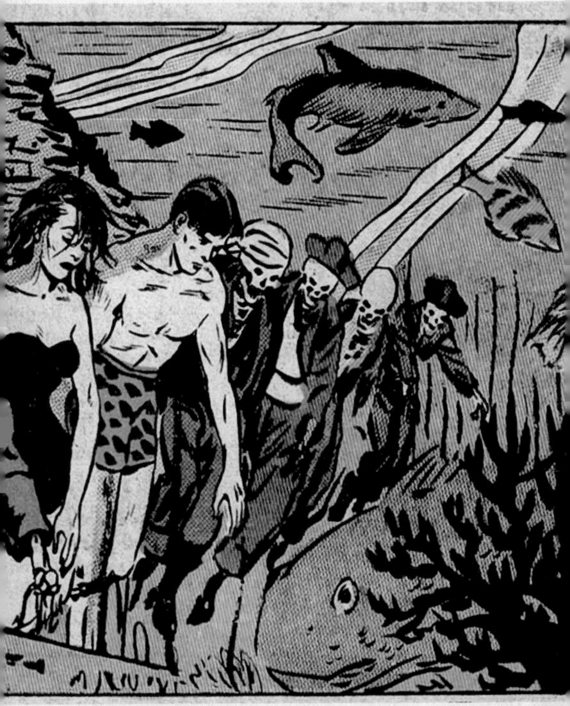

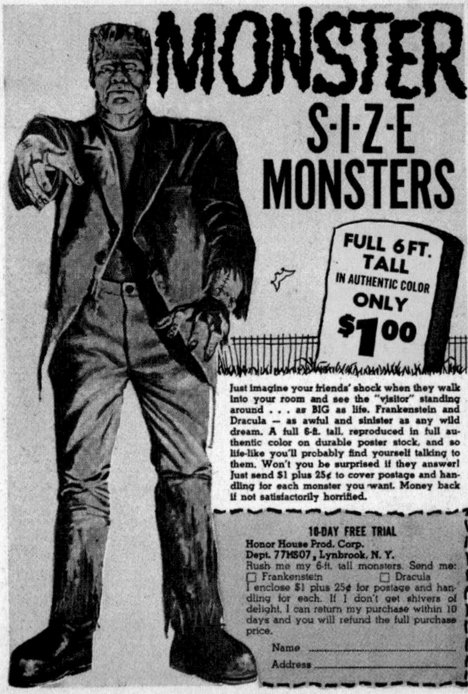
MONSTER
S-I-Z-E
MONSTERS
FULL 6 FT. TALL
IN AUTHENTIC COLOR
ONLY
$1.00
Just imagine your friends' shock when they walk into your room and see the "visitor" standing around . . . as BIG as life. Frankenstein and Dracula — as awful and sinister as any wild dream. A full 6-ft. tall, reproduced in full authentic color on durable poster stock, and so life-like you'll probably find yourself talking to them. Won't you be surprised if they answer! Just send $1 plus 25¢ to cover postage and handling for each monster you want. Money back if not satisfactorily horrified.
10-DAY FREE TRIAL
Honor House Prod. Corp.
Dept. 77MS07, Lynbrook, N. Y.
Rush me my 6-ft. tall monsters. Send me:
☐ Frankenstein ☐ Dracula
I enclose $1 plus 25¢ for postage and handling for each. If I don't get shivers of delight, I can return my purchase within 10 days and you will refund the full purchase price.
Name
Address

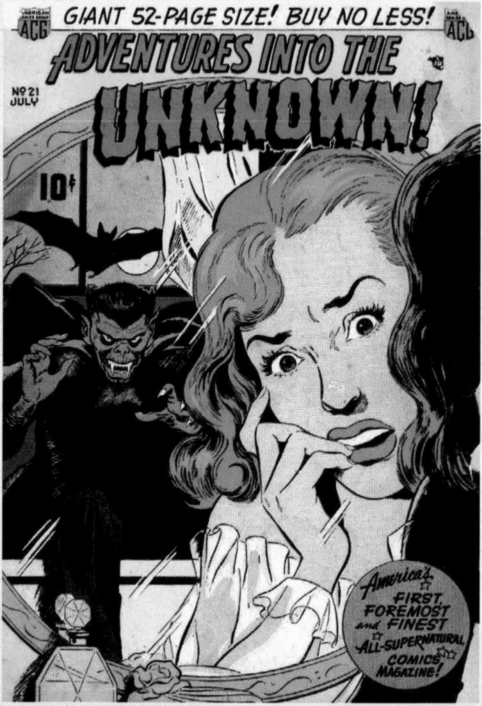
GIANT 52-PAGE SIZE! BUY NO LESS!
ACG
ACG
ADVENTURES INTO THE
UNKNOWN!
Nº 21
JULY
10¢
America's FIRST, FOREMOST and FINEST ALL-SUPERNATURAL COMICS MAGAZINE!

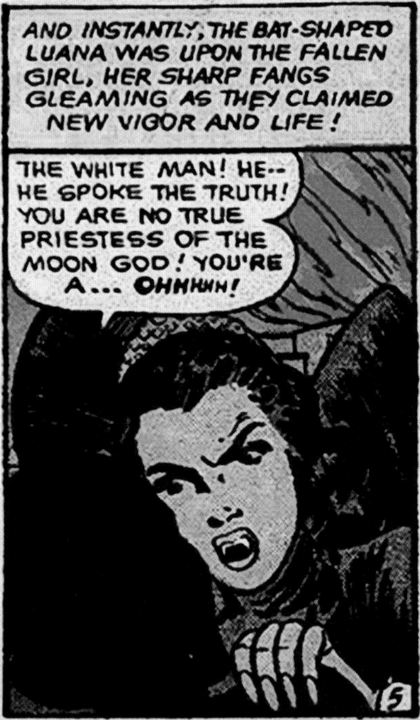
AND INSTANTLY, THE BAT-SHAPED LUANA WAS UPON THE FALLEN GIRL, HER SHARP FANGS GLEAMING AS THEY CLAIMED NEW VIGOR AND LIFE!
THE WHITE MAN! HE-- HE SPOKE THE TRUTH! YOU ARE NO TRUE PRIESTESS OF THE MOON GOD! YOU'RE A... OHHHHH!
5

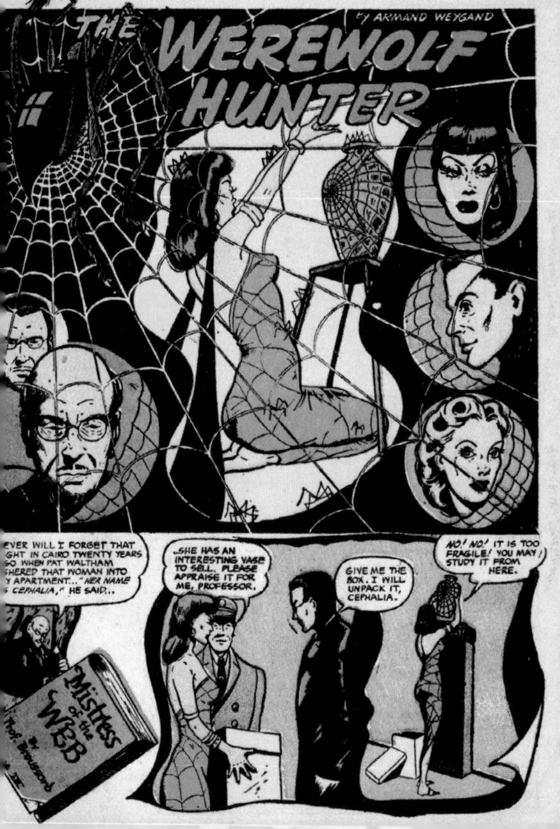
THE WEREWOLF HUNTER
by ARMAND WEYGAND
EVER WILL I FORGET THAT GHT IN CAIRO TWENTY YEARS GO WHEN PAT WALTHAM SHERED THAT WOMAN INTO Y APARTMENT..." "HER NAME S CEPHALIA," HE SAID...
Mistress of the WEB by Prof. Broussard
...SHE HAS AN INTERESTING VASE TO SELL. PLEASE APPRAISE IT FOR ME, PROFESSOR.
GIVE ME THE BOX. I WILL UNPACK IT, CEPHALIA.
NO! NO! IT IS TOO FRAGILE! YOU MAY STUDY IT FROM HERE.

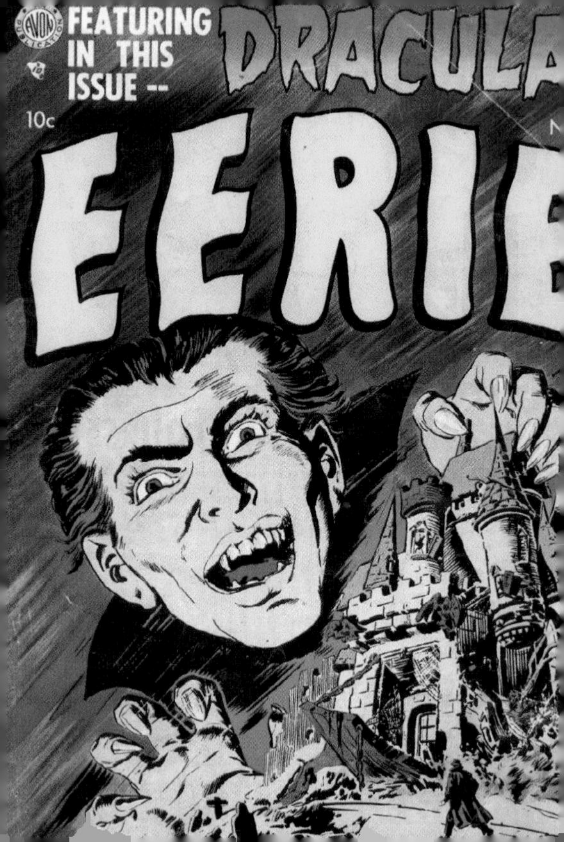
AVON PUBLICATION
FEATURING IN THIS ISSUE --
DRACULA
10c
EERIE

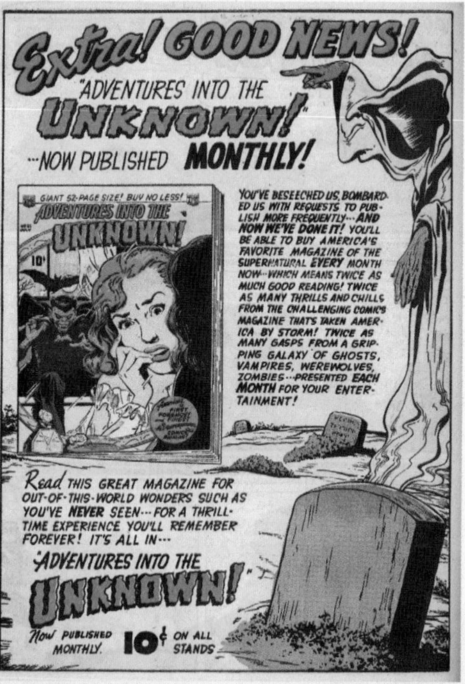
Extra! GOOD NEWS!
"ADVENTURES INTO THE UNKNOWN!"
...NOW PUBLISHED MONTHLY!
GIANT 52-PAGE SIZE! BUY NO LESS!
ADVENTURES INTO THE UNKNOWN!
10¢
YOU'VE BESEECHED US, BOMBARDED US WITH REQUESTS TO PUBLISH MORE FREQUENTLY... AND NOW WE'VE DONE IT! YOU'LL BE ABLE TO BUY AMERICA'S FAVORITE MAGAZINE OF THE SUPERNATURAL EVERY MONTH NOW...WHICH MEANS TWICE AS MUCH GOOD READING! TWICE AS MANY THRILLS AND CHILLS FROM THE CHALLENGING COMICS MAGAZINE THAT'S TAKEN AMERICA BY STORM! TWICE AS MANY GASPS FROM A GRIPPING GALAXY OF GHOSTS, VAMPIRES, WEREWOLVES, ZOMBIES...PRESENTED EACH MONTH FOR YOUR ENTERTAINMENT!
Read THIS GREAT MAGAZINE FOR OUT-OF-THIS-WORLD WONDERS SUCH AS YOU'VE NEVER SEEN...FOR A THRILL-TIME EXPERIENCE YOU'LL REMEMBER FOREVER! IT'S ALL IN...
"ADVENTURES INTO THE UNKNOWN!"
Now PUBLISHED MONTHLY.
10¢ ON ALL STANDS

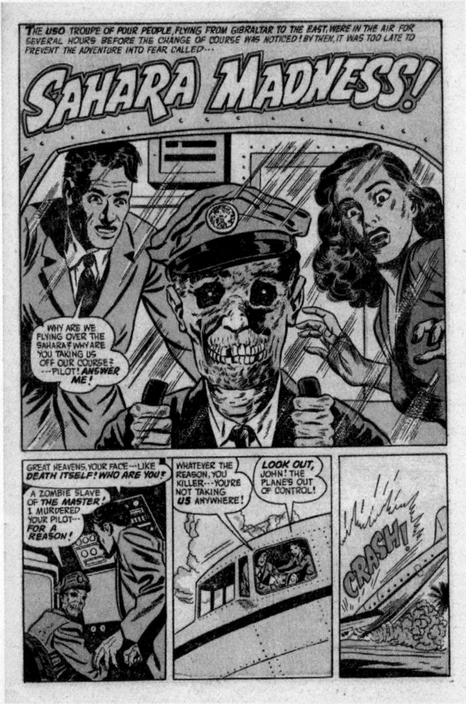
THE USO TROUPE OF FOUR PEOPLE, FLYING FROM GIBRALTAR TO THE EAST, WERE IN THE AIR FOR SEVERAL HOURS BEFORE THE CHANGE OF COURSE WAS NOTICED! BY THEN, IT WAS TOO LATE TO PREVENT THE ADVENTURE INTO FEAR CALLED---
SAHARA MADNESS!
WHY ARE WE FLYING OVER THE SAHARA? WHY ARE YOU TAKING US OFF OUR COURSE? ---PILOT! ANSWER ME!
GREAT HEAVENS, YOUR FACE---LIKE DEATH ITSELF! WHO ARE YOU?
A ZOMBIE SLAVE OF THE MASTER! I MURDERED YOUR PILOT--- FOR A REASON!
WHATEVER THE REASON, YOU KILLER---YOU'RE NOT TAKING US ANYWHERE!
LOOK OUT, JOHN! THE PLANE'S OUT OF CONTROL!
CRASH!

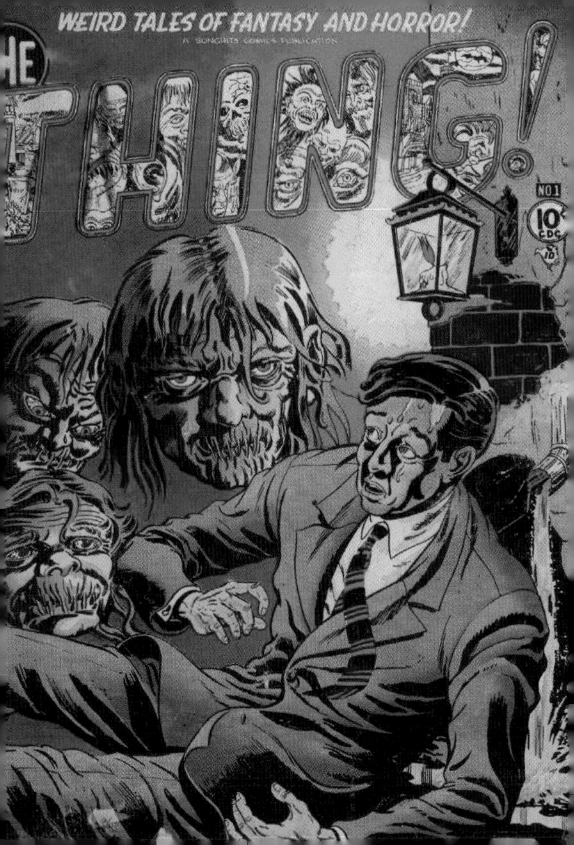
WEIRD TALES OF FANTASY AND HORROR!
A SONGHITS COMICS PUBLICATION
THE THING!
NO 1
10¢ CDC

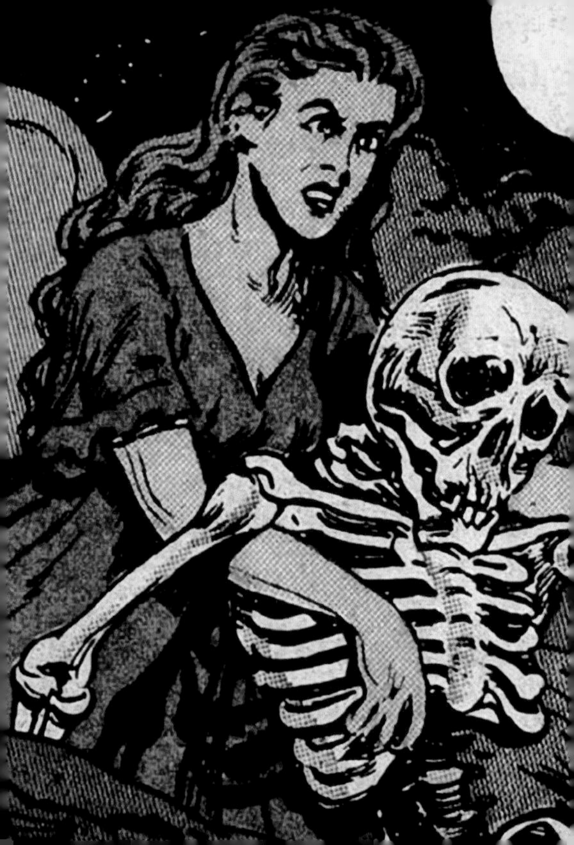

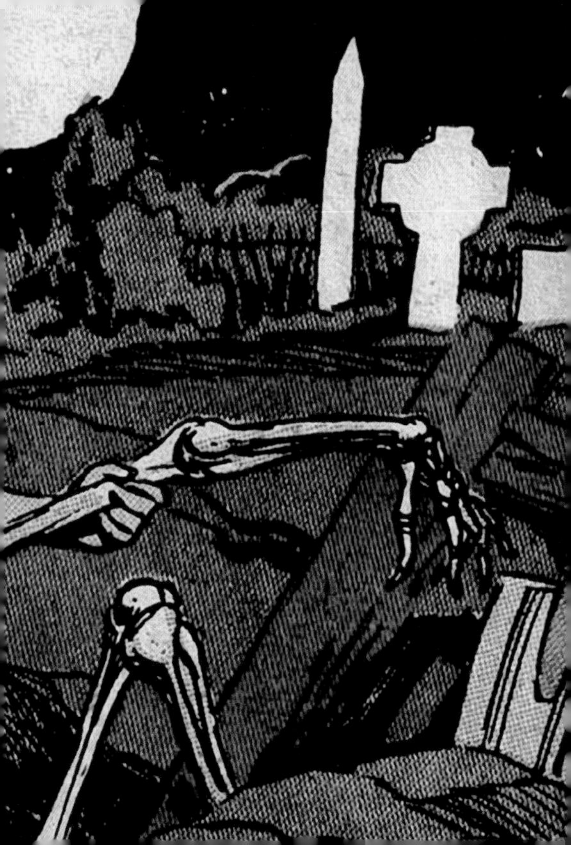

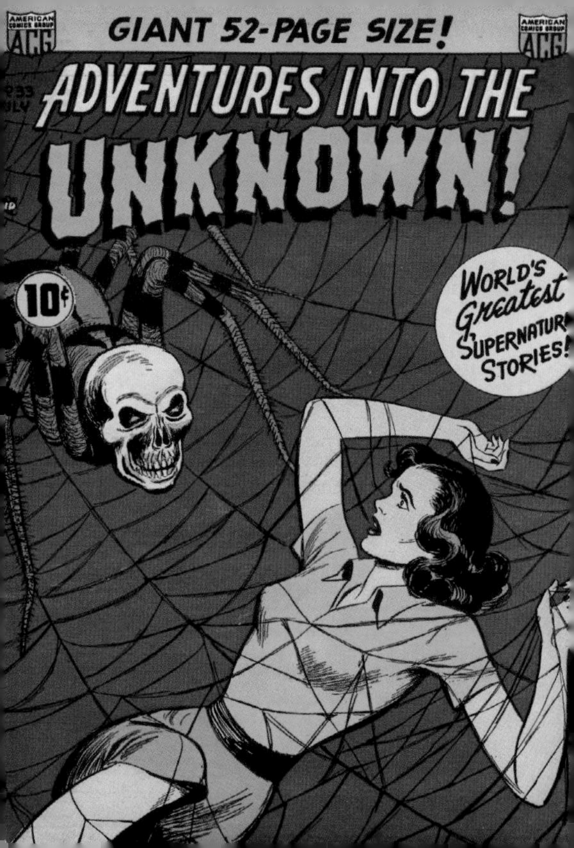

GIANT 52-PAGE SIZE!
ADVENTURES INTO THE UNKNOWN!
10¢
WORLD'S Greatest SUPERNATUR STORIES!

GALLERY

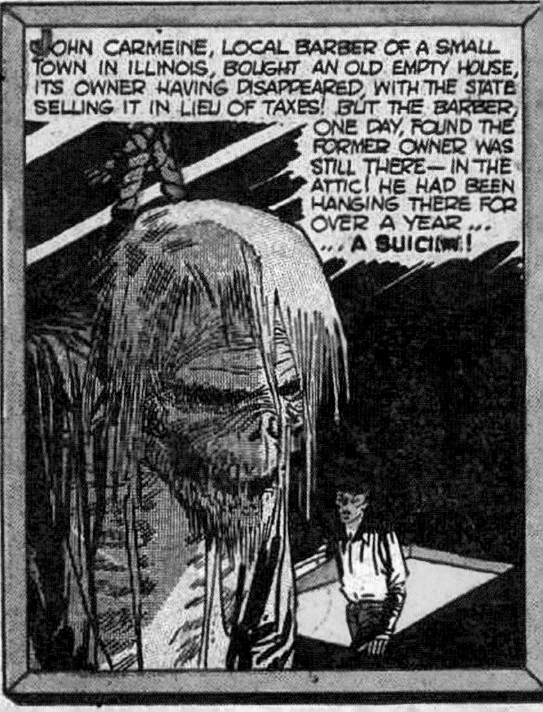
JOHN CARMEINE, LOCAL BARBER OF A SMALL TOWN IN ILLINOIS, BOUGHT AN OLD EMPTY HOUSE, ITS OWNER HAVING DISAPPEARED, WITH THE STATE SELLING IT IN LIEU OF TAXES! BUT THE BARBER, ONE DAY, FOUND THE FORMER OWNER WAS STILL THERE— IN THE ATTIC! HE HAD BEEN HANGING THERE FOR OVER A YEAR...
...A SUICI

F HORROR

B-1852

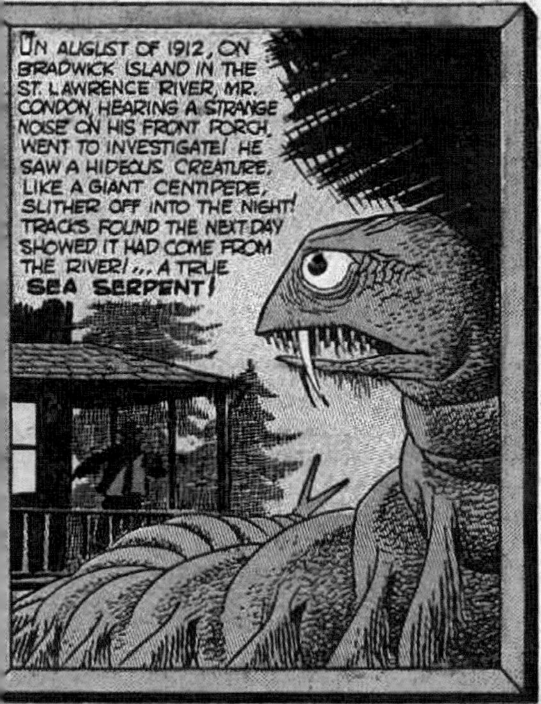
IN AUGUST OF 1912, ON BRADWICK ISLAND IN THE ST. LAWRENCE RIVER, MR. CONDON, HEARING A STRANGE NOISE ON HIS FRONT PORCH, WENT TO INVESTIGATE! HE SAW A HIDEOUS CREATURE, LIKE A GIANT CENTIPEDE, SLITHER OFF INTO THE NIGHT! TRACKS FOUND THE NEXT DAY SHOWED IT HAD COME FROM THE RIVER! ... A TRUE SEA SERPENT!

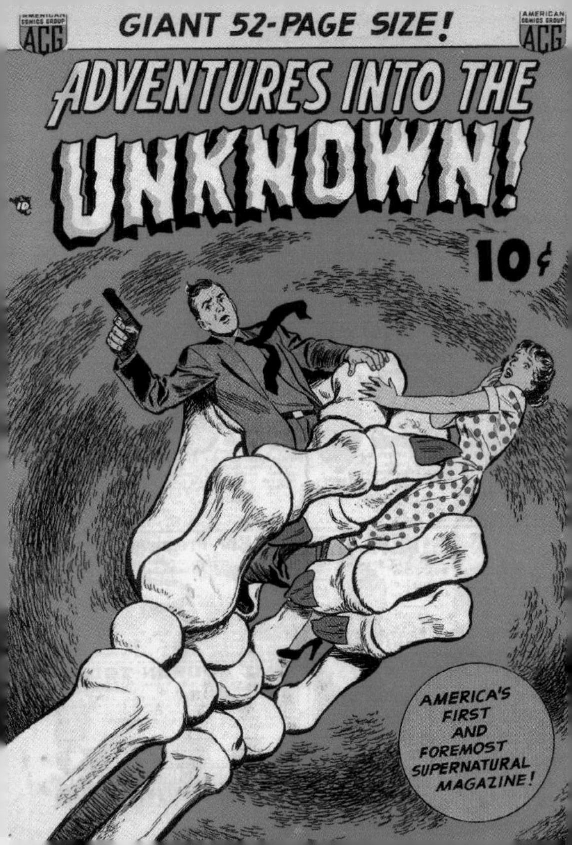
AMERICAN COMICS GROUP
ACG
GIANT 52-PAGE SIZE!
AMERICAN COMICS GROUP
ACG
ADVENTURES INTO THE
UNKNOWN!
10¢
AMERICA'S
FIRST
AND
FOREMOST
SUPERNATURAL
MAGAZINE!

The Man Who Died Twice

THERE have been many baffling and mysterious deaths recorded in the annals of the New York police; but from the entire list, one case stands out as a prime example of mystification. This was the case of the man who died twice, by suicide *and* murder!

Two distinct causes of death were involved, either one of which would have brought the victim's life to a speedy and unnatural end; yet the examining physician was unable to determine which condition was responsible. Nor were the police ever able to find any clues leading to the murderer—if it actually was a homicide. In brief, the case was a puzzle to end all murder puzzles: a fantastic mystery that nobody has ever solved.

It began in a tenement near Thirty-third Street and Second Avenue, where two men in their forties shared a bedroom on the top floor. The men were respectable laborers with no known enemies and no police records.

One morning the janitor of the tenement discovered one of these roomers dead in bed, already stiff and cold with rigor mortis. The examining police, as soon as they were summoned, found the corpse clad only in the lower portion of a pair of cheap pajamas. There was a small caliber bullet hole in the dead man's skull, the slug having passed through his head and stopped deep in the pillow.

The medical examiner would have thought no more of the case except for the fact that there was a long rubber tube in the mouth of the corpse, the other end attached to a gas jet nearby. Oddly enough, however, the gas was turned off and there was no odor of gas in the room. But there *was* a woman's green hat on the floor—if that meant anything.

A search of the room finally disclosed a revolver in a bureau drawer. The weapon had been fired once, and the ballistics experts matched the bullet in the pillow with the rifling of the revolver barrel. This was undoubtedly the death-gun. But who, after using it, had placed it in the bureau drawer? Not the dead man, for it was quite obvious that the wound in his head had caused instantaneous death.

Moreover, an autopsy revealed that the slug had entered his skull while he was still alive. Ordinarily this would have meant an open-and-shut case of murder. But further autopsy tests showed a fifty-seven percent saturation of gas in the blood, indicating that the man had inhaled enough gas through the rubber tube to have caused quick death. The question was: which had killed him, the gas or the bullet?

If he died of gas, he must have inhaled it after the bullet had penetrated his brain, and then got up from bed to turn off the petcock. This was a physical impossibility. On the other hand, if the bullet had killed him, then how could he have lived long enough to inhale lethal quantities of gas?

If he was a suicide, who had put the gun in the drawer and turned off the gas jet? If he was murdered by the gunshot wound, how could the killer have pumped gas into his dead lungs and bloodstream? To all appearances, the man had died twice, of two separate and distinct causes; yet each cause was sufficient, in itself, to have produced death.

The roommate was arrested but established an iron-clad alibi. The identity of the woman who owned the green hat was never discovered. And to this day, the New York police have a case on their hands which may never be fully explained.

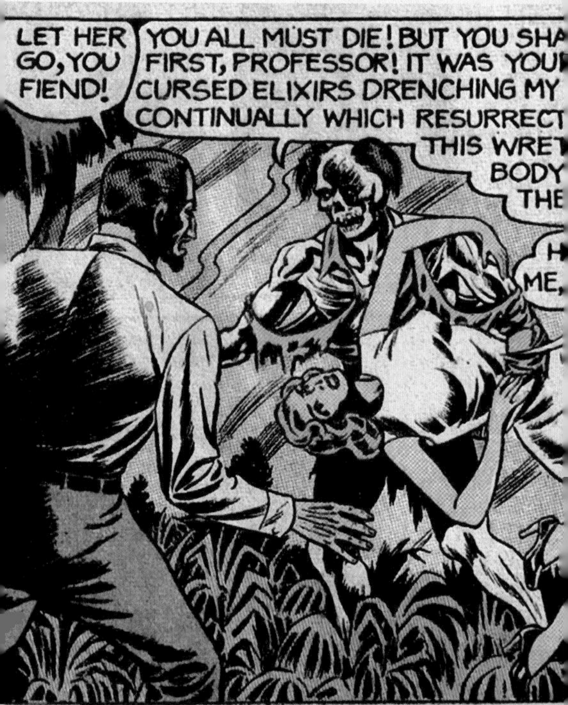
LET HER GO, YOU FIEND!
YOU ALL MUST DIE! BUT YOU SHA FIRST, PROFESSOR! IT WAS YOU CURSED ELIXIRS DRENCHING MY CONTINUALLY WHICH RESURRECT THIS WRET BODY THE
ME,

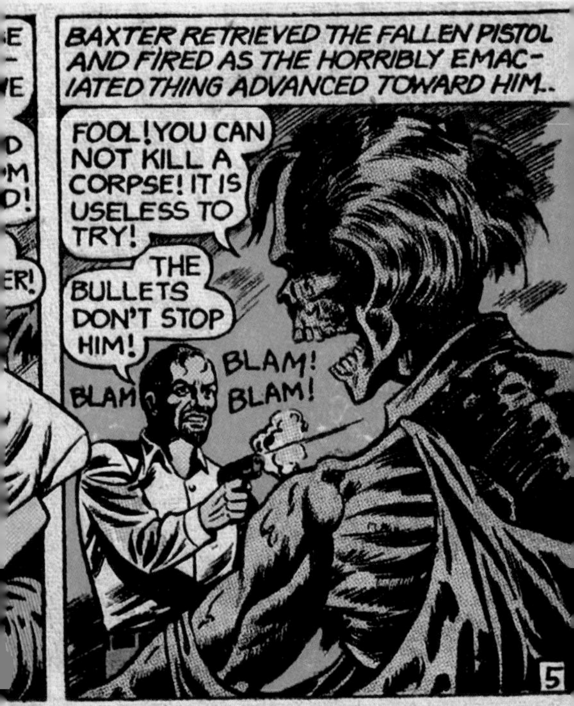
BAXTER RETRIEVED THE FALLEN PISTOL AND FIRED AS THE HORRIBLY EMACIATED THING ADVANCED TOWARD HIM..
FOOL! YOU CAN NOT KILL A CORPSE! IT IS USELESS TO TRY!
THE BULLETS DON'T STOP HIM!
BLAM
BLAM!
BLAM!
5

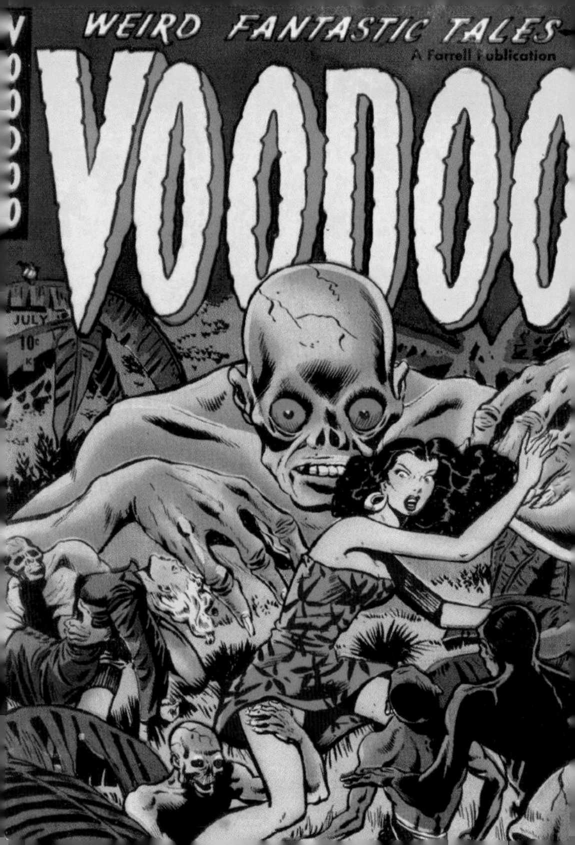
WEIRD FANTASTIC TALES
A Farrell Publication
VOODOO
JULY
10¢

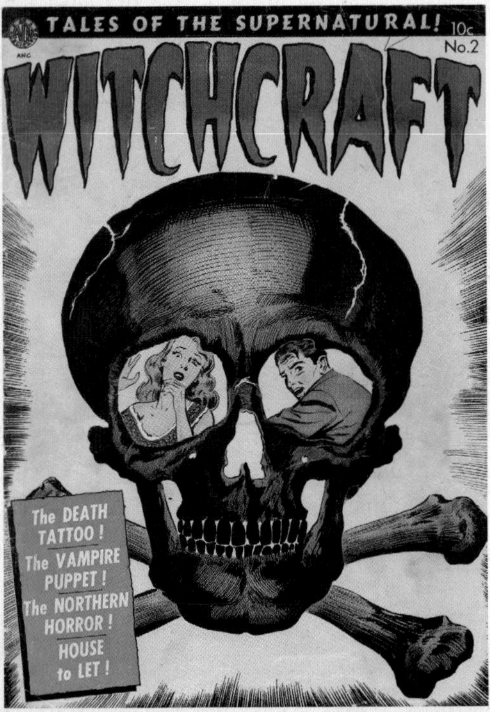
TALES OF THE SUPERNATURAL!
10c
No.2
ACG
WITCHCRAFT
The DEATH TATTOO!
The VAMPIRE PUPPET!
The NORTHERN HORROR!
HOUSE to LET!

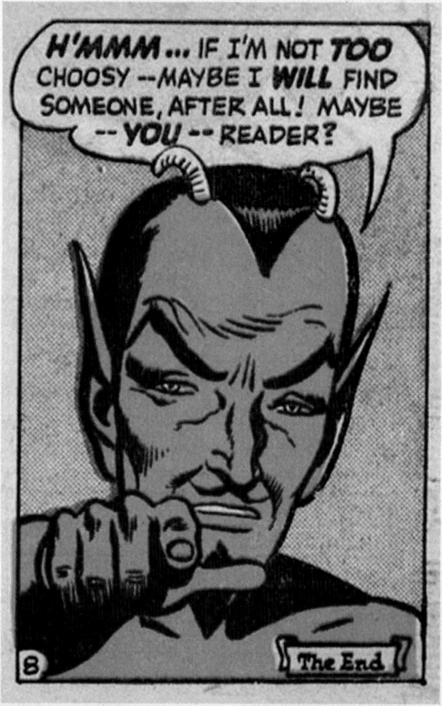
H'MMM... IF I'M NOT TOO CHOOSY --MAYBE I WILL FIND SOMEONE, AFTER ALL! MAYBE --YOU-- READER?
8
The End